This Crowde

Robert Bloch

Alpha Editions

This edition published in 2023

ISBN : 9789357946650

Design and Setting By
Alpha Editions
www.alphaedis.com
Email - info@alphaedis.com

Contents

1. Harry Collins—1997

The telescreen lit up promptly at eight a.m. Smiling Brad came on with his usual greeting. "Good morning—it's a beautiful day in Chicagee!"

Harry Collins rolled over and twitched off the receiver. "This I doubt," he muttered. He sat up and reached into the closet for his clothing.

Visitors—particularly feminine ones—were always exclaiming over the advantages of Harry's apartment. "So convenient," they would say. "Everything handy, right within reach. And think of all the extra steps you save!"

Of course most of them were just being polite and trying to cheer Harry up. They knew damned well that he wasn't living in one room through any choice of his own. The Housing Act was something you just couldn't get around; not in Chicagee these days. A bachelor was entitled to one room—no more and no less. And even though Harry was making a speedy buck at the agency, he couldn't hope to beat the regulations.

There was only one way to beat them and that was to get married. Marriage would automatically entitle him to two rooms—*if* he could find them someplace.

More than a few of his feminine visitors had hinted at just that, but Harry didn't respond. Marriage was no solution, the way he figured it. He knew that he couldn't hope to locate a two-room apartment any closer than eighty miles away. It was bad enough driving forty miles to and from work every morning and night without doubling the distance. If he did find a bigger place, that would mean a three-hour trip each way on one of the commutrains, and the commutrains were murder. The Black Hole of Calcutta, on wheels.

But then, everything was murder, Harry reflected, as he stepped from the toilet to the sink, from the sink to the stove, from the stove to the table.

Powdered eggs for breakfast. That was murder, too. But it was a fast, cheap meal, easy to prepare, and the ingredients didn't waste a lot of storage space. The only trouble was, he hated the way they tasted. Harry wished he had time to eat his breakfasts in a restaurant. He could afford the price, but he couldn't afford to wait in line more than a half-hour or so. His office schedule at the agency started promptly at ten-thirty. And he didn't get out until three-thirty; it was a long, hard five-hour day. Sometimes he wished he worked in the New Philly area, where a four-hour day was the rule. But he supposed that wouldn't mean any real saving in time, because he'd have to live further out. What was the population in New Philly now? Something like 63,000,000, wasn't it? Chicagee was much smaller—only 38,000,000, this year.

This year. Harry shook his head and took a gulp of the Instantea. Yes, this year the population was 38,000,000, and the boundaries of the community extended north to what used to be the old Milwaukee and south past Gary. What would it be like *next* year, and the year following?

Lately that question had begun to haunt Harry. He couldn't quite figure out why. After all, it was none of his business, really. He had a good job, security, a nice place just two hours from the Loop. He even drove his own car. What more could he ask?

And why did he have to start the day like this, with a blinding headache?

Harry finished his Instantea and considered the matter. Yes, it was beginning again, just as it had on almost every morning for the past month. He'd sit down at the table, eat his usual breakfast, and end up with a headache. Why?

It wasn't the food; for a while he'd deliberately varied his diet, but that didn't make any difference. And he'd had his usual monthly checkup not more than ten days ago, only to be assured there was nothing wrong with him. Still, the headaches persisted. Every morning, when he'd sit down and jerk his head to the left like this—

That was it. Jerking his head to the left. It always seemed to trigger the pain. But why? And where had he picked up this habit of jerking his head to the left?

Harry didn't know.

He glanced at his watch. It was almost nine, now. High time that he got started. He reached over to the interapartment video and dialled the garage downstairs.

"Bill," he said. "Can you bring my car around to Number Three?"

The tiny face in the hand-screen grinned sheepishly. "Mr. Collins, ain't it? Gee, I'm sorry, Mr. Collins. Night crew took on a new man, he must have futzed around with the lists, and I can't find your number."

Harry sighed. "It's one-eight-seven-three-dash-five," he said. "Light blue Pax, two-seater. Do you want the license number, too?"

"No, just your parking number. I'll recognize it when I see it. But God only knows what level it's on. That night man really—"

"Never mind," Harry interrupted. "How soon?"

"Twenty minutes or so. Maybe half an hour."

"Half an hour? I'll be late. Hurry it up!"

Harry clicked the video and shook his head. Half an hour! Well, you had to expect these things if you wanted to be independent and do your own driving today. If he wanted to work his priority through the office, he could get his application honored on the I.C. Line within a month. But the I.C. was just another commutrain, and he couldn't take it. Standing and swaying for almost two hours, fighting the crowds, battling his way in and out of the sidewalk escalators. Besides, there was always the danger of being crushed. He'd seen an old man trampled to death on a Michigan Boulevard escalator-feeder, and he'd never forgotten it.

Being afraid was only a partial reason for his reluctance to change. The worst thing, for Harry, was the thought of all those people; the forced bodily contact, the awareness of smothered breathing, odors, and the crushing confinement of flesh against flesh. It was bad enough in the lines, or on the streets. The commutrain was just too much.

Yet, as a small boy, Harry could remember the day when he'd loved such trips. Sitting there looking out of the window as the scenery whirled past—that was always a thrill when you were a little kid. How long ago had that been? More than twenty years, wasn't it?

Now there weren't any seats, and no windows. Which was just as well, probably, because the scenery didn't whirl past any more, either. Instead, there was a stop at every station on the line, and a constant battle as people jockeyed for position to reach the exit-doors in time.

No, the car was better.

Harry reached for a container in the cabinet and poured out a couple of aspirystamines. That ought to help the headache. At least until he got to the office. Then he could start with the daily quota of yellowjackets. Meanwhile, getting out on the street might help him, too. A shame there wasn't a window in this apartment, but then, what good would it do, really? All he could see through it would be the next apartment.

He shrugged and picked up his coat. Nine-thirty, time to go downstairs. Maybe the car would be located sooner than Bill had promised; after all, he had nine assistants, and not everybody went to work on this first daylight shift.

Harry walked down the hall and punched the elevator button. He looked at the indicator, watched the red band move towards the numeral of this floor, then sweep past it.

"Full up!" he muttered. "Oh, well."

He reached out and touched both sides of the corridor. That was another thing he disliked; these narrow corridors. Two people could scarcely squeeze past one another without touching. Of course, it did save space to build apartments this way, and space was at a premium. But Harry couldn't get used to it. Now he remembered some of the old buildings that were still around when he was a little boy—

The headache seemed to be getting worse instead of better. Harry looked at the indicator above the other elevator entrance. The red band was crawling upward, passing him to stop on 48. That was the top floor. Now it was moving down, down; stopping on 47, 46, 45, 44, 43, and—here it was!

"Stand back, please!" said the tape. Harry did his best to oblige, but there wasn't much room. A good two dozen of his upstairs neighbors jammed the compartment. Harry thought he recognized one or two of the men, but he couldn't be sure. There were so many people, so many faces. After a while it got so they all seemed to look alike. Yes, and breathed alike, and felt alike when you were squeezed up against them, and you were always being squeezed up against them, wherever you went. And you could smell them, and hear them wheeze and cough, and you went falling down with them into a bottomless pit where your head began to throb and throb and it was hard to move away from all that heat and pressure. It was hard enough just to keep from screaming—

Then the door opened and Harry was catapulted out into the lobby. The mob behind him pushed and clawed because they were in a hurry; they were always in a hurry these days, and if you got in their way they'd trample you down like that old man had been trampled down; there was no room for one man in a crowd any more.

Harry blinked and shook his head.

He gripped the edge of the wall and clung there in an effort to avoid being swept out of the lobby completely. His hands were sticky with perspiration. They slipped off as he slowly inched his way back through the crush of the mob.

"Wait for me!" he called. "Wait for me, I'm going down!" But his voice was lost in the maelstrom of sound just as his body was lost in the maelstrom of motion. Besides, an automatic elevator cannot hear. It is merely a mechanism that goes up and down, just like the other mechanisms that go in and out, or around and around, and you get caught up in them the way a squirrel gets caught in a squirrel-cage and you race and race, and the best you can hope for is to keep up with the machinery.

The elevator door clanged shut before Harry could reach it. He waited for another car to arrive, and this time he stood aside as the crowd emerged, then darted in behind them.

The car descended to the first garage level, and Harry stood gulping gratefully in the comparative isolation. There weren't more than ten people accompanying him.

He emerged on the ramp, gave his number to the attendant, and waved at Bill in his office. Bill seemed to recognize him; at least he nodded, briefly. No sense trying to talk—not in this sullen subterranea, filled with the booming echo of exhausts, the despairing shriek of brakes. Headlights flickered in the darkness as cars whirled past, ascending and descending on the loading platforms. The signal systems winked from the walls, and tires screeched defiance to the warning bells.

Old-fashioned theologians, Harry remembered, used to argue whether there really was a Hell, and if so, had it been created by God or the Devil? Too bad they weren't around today to get an answer to their questions. There *was* a Hell, and it had been created by General Motors.

Harry's temples began to throb. Through blurred eyes, he saw the attendant beckoning him down the line to a platform marked *Check-Out #3*. He stood there with a cluster of others, waiting.

What was the matter with him today, anyway? First the headache, and now his feet were hurting. Standing around waiting, that's what did it. This eternal waiting. When he was a kid, the grownups were always complaining about the long seven-hour work days and how they cut into their leisure time. Well, maybe they had reason to gripe, but at least there *was* some leisure before work began or after it was through. Now that extra time was consumed in waiting. Standing in line, standing in crowds, wearing yourself out doing nothing.

Still, this time it wasn't really so bad. Within ten minutes the light blue Pax rolled up before him. Harry climbed in as the attendant slid out from behind the wheel and prepared to leave.

Then a fat man appeared, running along the ramp. He gestured wildly with a plump thumb. Harry nodded briefly, and the fat man hurled himself into the seat beside him and slammed the door.

They were off. Harry read the signals impatiently, waiting for the green *Go*. The moment he saw it he gunned his motor and got the car up to twenty-two and zipped away.

That's what he liked, that's what he always waited for. Of course it was dangerous, here in the tunnel system under the garage, but Harry always got a thrill out of speed. The Pax could do thirty-five or even forty, probably, on a theoretical open road. Still, twenty-two was enough to satisfy Harry.

He whizzed up the ramp, turned, headed for the street-level, then braked and waited for the signal to emerge.

Harsh sunlight pierced the smog and he felt his eyes watering. Now the street noises assailed his ears; the grinding of gears, the revving of motors. But at least the total volume was lower, and with the windows tightly closed against the acrid air, he could hear.

Turning to the fat man beside him he said, "Hello, Frazer. What's the urgency?"

"Got to get downtown before eleven," the fat man answered. "Board meeting today, but I forgot about it. Knew I wouldn't have time to wait for the car, and I was hoping I'd find someone who'd give me a lift. Lucky for me that you came along when you did."

Harry nodded but did not reply. At the moment he was trying to edge into the traffic beyond. It flowed, bumper to bumper, in a steady stream; a stream moving at the uniform and prescribed rate of fifteen miles per hour. He released his brakes and the Pax nosed forward until a truck sounded its horn in ominous warning. The noise hurt Harry's head; he winced and grimaced.

"What's the matter?" asked Frazer.

"Headache," Harry muttered. He menaced a Chevsoto with his bumper. "Damn it, I thought they didn't allow those big four-passenger jobs on this arterial during rush hours!" Gradually he managed to turn until he was in the righthand lane. "There," he said. "We're off."

And so they were, for all of three minutes, with the speed set at fifteen on autopilot. Then a signal went into action somewhere up ahead, and the procession halted. Harry flicked his switch. As was customary, horns sounded indignantly on all sides—a mechanical protest against a mechanical obstruction. Harry winced again.

"Hangover?" Frazer asked, solicitously. "Try aspirystamine."

Harry shook his head. "No hangover. And I've already taken three, thanks. Nothing does any good. So I guess it's just up to you."

"Up to me?" Frazer was genuinely puzzled. "What can I do about your headaches?"

"You're on the Board of City Planners, aren't you?"

"That's right."

"Well, I've got a suggestion for you to give to them. Tell them to start planning to drop a couple of heavy thermo-nucs on this area. Clean out twenty or thirty million people. We'd never miss 'em."

Frazer chuckled wryly. "I wish I had a buck for every time I've heard *that* suggestion."

"Ever stop to think why you hear it so often? It's because everybody feels the same way—we can't take being hemmed in like this."

"Well, a bomb wouldn't help. You know that." Frazer pursed his lips. "Robertson figured out what would happen, with the chain-reaction."

Harry glanced sideways at his companion as the car started forward once again. "I've always wondered about that," he said. "Seriously, I mean. Is the story really true, or is it just some more of this government propaganda you fellows like to hand out?"

Frazer sighed. "It's true, all right. There was a scientist named Robertson, and he did come up with the thermo-nuc formula, way back in '75. Proved it, too. Use what he developed and the chain-reaction would never end. Scientists in other countries tested the theory and agreed; there was no collusion, it just worked out that way on a practical basis. Hasn't been a war since—what more proof do you want?"

"Well, couldn't they just use some of the old-fashioned hydrogen bombs?"

"Be sensible, man! Once a war started, no nation could resist the temptation to go all-out. Fortunately, everyone realizes that. So we have peace. Permanent peace."

"I'll take a good war anytime, in preference to this."

"Harry, you don't know what you're talking about. You aren't so young that you can't remember what it was like in the old days. Everybody living in fear, waiting for the bombs to fall. People dying of disease and worried about dying from radiation and fallout. All the international rivalries, the power-politics, the eternal pressures and constant crises. Nobody in his right mind would want to go back to *that*. We've come a mighty long way in the last twenty years or so."

Harry switched to autopilot and sat back. "Maybe that's the trouble," he said. "Maybe we've come too far, too fast. I wasn't kidding about dropping those thermo-nucs, either. *Something* has to be done. We can't go on like this indefinitely. Why doesn't the Board come up with an answer?"

Frazer shrugged his heavy shoulders. "You think we haven't tried, aren't trying now? We're aware of the situation as well as you are—and then some. But there's no easy solution. The population just keeps growing, that's all. No war to cut it down, contagious diseases at a minimum, average life-expectancy up to ninety years or better. Naturally, this results in a problem.

But a bomb won't help bring about any permanent solution. Besides, this isn't a local matter, or even a national one. It's global. What do you think those summit meetings are all about?"

"What about birth control?" Harry asked. "Why don't they really get behind an emigration movement?"

"We can't limit procreation by law. You know that." Frazer peered out at the swarming streams on the sidewalk levels. "It's more than a religious or a political question—it's a social one. People want kids. They can afford them. Besides, the Housing Act is set up so that having kids is just about the only way you can ever get into larger living-quarters."

"Couldn't they try reverse-psychology? I mean, grant priority to people who are willing to be sterilized?"

"They tried it, on a limited experimental scale, about three years ago out on the West Coast."

"I never heard anything about it."

"Damned right you didn't," Frazer replied, grimly. "They kept the whole project under wraps, and for a good reason. The publicity might have wrecked the Administration."

"What happened?"

"What do you suppose happened? There were riots. Do you think a man and his wife and three kids, living in three rooms, liked the idea of standing by and watching a sterilized couple enjoy a four-room place with lawn space? Things got pretty ugly, let me tell you. There was a rumor going around that the country was in the hands of homosexuals—the churches were up in arms—and if that wasn't bad enough, we had to face up to the primary problem. There just wasn't, just isn't, enough *space*. Not in areas suitable for maintaining a population. Mountains are still mountains and deserts are still deserts. Maybe we can put up housing in such regions, but who can live there? Even with decentralization going full blast, people must live within reasonable access to their work. No, we're just running out of room."

Again the car halted on signal. Over the blasting of the horns, Harry repeated his query about emigration.

Frazer shook his head, but made no attempt to reply until the horns had quieted and they were under way once more.

"As for emigration, we're just getting some of our own medicine in return. About eighty years ago, we clamped down and closed the door on immigrants; established a quota. Now the same quota is being used against us, and you can't really blame other nations for it. They're facing worse population increases than we are. Look at the African Federation, and what's happened there, in spite of all the wealth! And South America is even worse, in spite of all the reclamation projects. Fifteen years ago, when they cleared out the Amazon Basin, they thought they'd have enough room for fifty years to come. And now look at it--two hundred million, that's the latest figure we've got."

"So what's the answer?" Harry asked.

"I don't know. If it wasn't for hydroponics and the Ag Culture controls, we'd be licked right now. As it is, we can still supply enough food, and the old supply-and-demand takes care of the economy as a whole. I have no recommendations for an overall solution, or even a regional one. My job, the Board's job, is regulating housing and traffic and transportation in Chicagee. That's about all you can expect us to handle."

Again they jolted to a stop and the horns howled all around them. Harry sat there until a muscle in the side of his jaw began to twitch. Suddenly he pounded on the horn with both fists.

"Shut up!" he yelled. "For the love of Heaven, shut up!"

Abruptly he slumped back. "Sorry," he mumbled. "It's my damned headache. I—I've got to get out of this."

"Job getting you down?"

"No. It's a good job. At least everybody tells me so. Twenty-five hours a week, three hundred bucks. The car. The room. The telescreen and liquor and yellowjackets. Plenty of time to kill. Unless it's the time that's killing me."

"But—what do you *want*?"

Harry stepped on the accelerator and they inched along. Now the street widened into eight traffic lanes and the big semis joined the procession on the edge of the downtown area.

"I want out," Harry said. "Out of this."

"Don't you ever visit the National Preserves?" Frazer asked.

"Sure I do. Fly up every vacation. Take a tame plane to a tame government resort and catch my quota of two tame fish. Great sport! If I got married, I'd be entitled to four tame fish. But that's not what I want. I want what my father used to talk about. I want to drive into the country, without a permit, mind you; just to drive wherever I like. I want to see cows and chickens and trees and lakes and sky."

"You sound like a Naturalist."

"Don't sneer. Maybe the Naturalists are right. Maybe we ought to cut out all this phoney progress and phoney peace that passeth all understanding. I'm no liberal, don't get me wrong, but sometimes I think the Naturalists have the only answer."

"But what can you do about it?" Frazer murmured. "Suppose for the sake of argument that they *are* right. How can you change things? We can't just *will* ourselves to stop growing, and we can't legislate against biology. More people, in better health, with more free time, are just bound to have more offspring. It's inevitable, under the circumstances. And neither you nor I nor anyone has the right to condemn millions upon millions of others to death through war or disease."

"I know," Harry said. "It's hopeless, I guess. All the same, I want out." He wet his lips. "Frazer, you're on the Board here. You've got connections higher up. If I could only get a chance to transfer to Ag Culture, go on one of those farms as a worker—"

Frazer shook his head. "Sorry, Harry. You know the situation there, I'm sure. Right now there's roughly ninety million approved applications on file. Everybody wants to get into Ag Culture."

"But couldn't I just buy some land, get a government contract for foodstuffs?"

"Have you got the bucks? A minimum forty acres leased from one of the farm corporations will cost you two hundred thousand at the very least, not counting equipment." He paused. "Besides, there's Vocational Apt. What did your tests show?"

"You're right," Harry said. "I'm supposed to be an agency man. An agency man until I die. Or retire on my pension, at fifty, and sit in my little room for the next fifty years, turning on the telescreen every morning to hear some loudmouthed liar tell me it's a beautiful day in Chicagee. Who knows, maybe by that time we'll have a hundred billion people enjoying peace and progress and prosperity. All sitting in little rooms and—"

"Watch out!" Frazer grabbed the wheel. "You nearly hit that truck." He waited until Harry's face relaxed before relinquishing his grip. "Harry, you'd better go in for a checkup. It isn't just a headache with you, is it?"

"You're not fooling," Harry told him. "It isn't just a headache."

He began to think about what it *really* was, and that helped a little. It helped him get through the worst part, which was the downtown traffic and letting Frazer off and listening to Frazer urge him to see a doctor.

Then he got to the building parking area and let them take his car away and bury it down in the droning darkness where the horns hooted and the headlights glared.

Harry climbed the ramp and mingled with the ten-thirty shift on its way up to the elevators. Eighteen elevators in his building, to serve eighty floors. Nine of the elevators were express to the fiftieth floor, three were express to sixty-five. He wanted one of the latter, and so did the mob. The crushing, clinging mob. They pressed and panted the way mobs always do; mobs that lynch and torture and dance around bonfires and guillotines and try to drag you down to trample you to death because they can't stand you if your name is Harry and you want to be different.

They hate you because you don't like powdered eggs and the telescreen and a beautiful day in Chicagee. And they stare at you because your forehead hurts and the muscle in your jaw twitches and they know you want to scream as you go up, up, up, and try to think why you get a headache from jerking your head to the left.

Then Harry was at the office door and they said good morning when he came in, all eighty of the typists in the outer office working their electronic machines and offering him their electronic smiles, including the girl he had made electronic love to last Saturday night and who wanted him to move into a two-room marriage and have children, lots of children who could enjoy peace and progress and prosperity.

Harry snapped out of it, going down the corridor. Only a few steps more and he'd be safe in his office, his own private office, almost as big as his apartment. And there would be liquor, and the yellowjackets in the drawer. That would help. Then he could get to work.

What was today's assignment? He tried to remember. It was Wilmer-Klibby, wasn't it? Telescreenads for Wilmer-Klibby, makers of window-glass.

Window-glass.

He opened his office door and then slammed it shut behind him. For a minute everything blurred, and then he could remember.

Now he knew what caused him to jerk his head, what gave him the headaches when he did so. Of course. That was it.

When he sat down at the table for breakfast in the morning he turned his head to the left because he'd always done so, ever since he was a little boy. A little boy, in what was then Wheaton, sitting at the breakfast table and looking out of the window. Looking out at summer sunshine, spring rain, autumn haze, the white wonder of newfallen snow.

He'd never broken himself of the habit. He still looked to the left every morning, just as he had today. But there was no window any more. There was only a blank wall. And beyond it, the smog and the clamor and the crowds.

Window-glass. Wilmer-Klibby had problems. Nobody was buying window-glass any more. Nobody except the people who put up buildings like this. There were still windows on the top floors, just like the window here in his office.

Harry stepped over to it, moving very slowly because of his head. It hurt to keep his eyes open, but he wanted to stare out of the window. Up this high you could see above the smog. You could see the sun like a radiant jewel packed in the cotton cumulus of clouds. If you opened the window you could feel fresh air against your forehead, you could breathe it in and breathe out the headache.

But you didn't dare look down. Oh, no, never look *down*, because then you'd see the buildings all around you. The buildings below, black and sooty, their jagged outlines like the stumps of rotten teeth. And they stretched off in all directions, as far as the eye could attain; row after row of rotten teeth grinning up from the smog-choked throat of the streets. From the maw of the city far below came this faint but endless howling, this screaming of traffic and toil. And you couldn't help it, you breathed *that* in too, along with the fresh air, and it poisoned you and it did more than make your head ache. It made your heart ache and it made your soul sick, and it made you close your eyes and your lungs and your brain against it.

Harry reeled, but he knew this was the only way. *Close your brain against it.* And then, when you opened your eyes again, maybe you could see the way things used to be—

It was snowing out and it was a *wet* snow, the very best kind for snowballs and making a snowman, and the whole gang would come out after school.

But there was no school, this was Saturday, and the leaves were russet and gold and red so that it looked as if all the trees in the world were on fire. And you could scuff when you walked and pile up fallen leaves from the grass and roll in them.

And it was swell to roll down the front lawn in summer, just roll right down to the edge of the sidewalk like it was a big hill and let Daddy catch you at the bottom, laughing.

Mamma laughed too, and she said, *Look, it's springtime, the lilacs are out, do you want to touch the pretty lilacs, Harry?*

And Harry didn't quite understand what she was saying, but he reached out and they were purple and smelled of rain and soft sweetness and they were just beyond the window, if he reached a little further he could touch them—

And then the snow and the leaves and the grass and the lilacs disappeared, and Harry could see the rotten teeth again, leering and looming and snapping at him. They were going to bite, they were going to chew, they were going to devour, and he couldn't stop them, couldn't stop himself. He was falling into the howling jaws of the city.

His last conscious effort was a desperate attempt to gulp fresh air into his lungs before he pinwheeled down. Fresh air was good for headaches....

---

2. Harry Collins—1998

It took them ten seconds to save Harry from falling, but it took him over ten weeks to regain his balance.

In fact, well over two months had passed before he could fully realize just what had happened, or where he was now. They must have noticed something was wrong with him that morning at the office, because two supervisors and an exec rushed in and caught him just as he was going out of the window. And then they had sent him away, sent him *here.*

"This is fine," he told Dr. Manschoff. "If I'd known how well they treated you, I'd have gone couch-happy years ago."

Dr. Manschoff's plump face was impassive, but the little laugh-lines deepened around the edges of his eyes. "Maybe that's why we take such care not to publicize our recent advances in mental therapy," he said. "Everybody would want to get into a treatment center, and then where would we be?"

Harry nodded, staring past the doctor's shoulder, staring out of the wide window at the broad expanse of rolling countryside beyond.

"I still don't understand, though," he murmured. "How can you possibly manage to maintain an institution like this, with all the space and the luxuries? The inmates seem to lead a better life than the adjusted individuals outside. It's topsy-turvy."

"Perhaps." Dr. Manschoff's fingers formed a pudgy steeple. "But then, so many things seem to be topsy-turvy nowadays, don't they? Wasn't it the realization of this fact which precipitated your own recent difficulties?"

"Almost precipitated me bodily out of that window," Harry admitted, cheerfully. "And that's another thing. I was sent here, I suppose, because I'd attempted suicide, gone into shock, temporary amnesia, something like that."

"Something like that," the doctor echoed, contemplating his steeple.

"But you didn't give me any treatment," Harry continued. "Oh, I was kept under sedation for a while, I realize that. And you and some of the other staff-members talked to me. But mainly I just rested in a nice big room and ate nice big meals."

"So?" The steeple's fleshy spire collapsed.

"So what I want to know is, when does the real treatment start? When do I go into analysis, or chemotherapy, and all that?"

Dr. Manschoff shrugged. "Do you think you need those things now?"

Harry gazed out at the sunlight beyond the window, half-squinting and half-frowning. "No, come to think of it, I don't believe I do. I feel better now than I have in years."

His companion leaned back. "Meaning that for years you felt all wrong. Because you were constricted, physically, psychically, and emotionally. You were cramped, squeezed in a vise until the pressure became intolerable. But now that pressure has been removed. As a result you no longer suffer, and there is no need to seek escape in death or denial of identity.

"This radical change of attitude has been brought about here in just a little more than two months' time. And yet you're asking me when the 'real treatment' begins."

"I guess I've already had the real treatment then, haven't I?"

"That is correct. Prolonged analysis or drastic therapy is unnecessary. We've merely given you what you seemed to need."

"I'm very grateful," Harry said. "But how can you afford to do it?"

Dr. Manschoff built another temple to an unknown god. He inspected the architecture critically now as he spoke. "Because your problem is a rarity," he said.

"Rarity? I'd have thought millions of people would be breaking down every month. The Naturalists say—"

The doctor nodded wearily. "I know what they say. But let's dismiss rumors and consider facts. Have you ever read any *official* report stating that the number of cases of mental illness ran into the millions?"

"No, I haven't."

"For that matter, do you happen to know of *anyone* who was ever sent to a treatment center such as this?"

"Well, of course, everybody goes in to see the medics for regular check-ups and this includes an interview with a psych. But if they're in bad shape he just puts them on extra tranquilizers. I guess sometimes he reviews their Vocational Apt tests and shifts them over into different jobs in other areas."

Dr. Manschoff bowed his head in reverence above the steeple, as if satisfied with the labors he had wrought. "That is roughly correct. And I believe, if you search your memory, you won't recall even a mention of a treatment center. This sort of place is virtually extinct, nowadays. There are still some institutions for those suffering from functional mental disorders—paresis, senile dementia, congenital abnormalities. But regular check-ups and preventative therapy take care of the great majority. We've ceased concentrating on the result of mental illnesses and learned to attack the causes.

"It's the old yellow fever problem all over again, you see. Once upon a time, physicians dealt exclusively with treatment of yellow fever patients. Then they shifted their attention to the *source* of the disease. They went after the mosquitoes, drained the swamps, and the yellow fever problem vanished.

"That's been our approach in recent years. We've developed *social* therapy, and so the need for individual therapy has diminished.

"What were the sources of the tensions producing mental disturbances? Physical and financial insecurity, the threat of war, the aggressive patterns of a competitive society, the unresolved Oedipus-situation rooted in the old-style family relationship. These were the swamps where the mosquitoes buzzed and bit. Most of the swamps have been dredged, most of the insects exterminated.

"Today we're moving into a social situation where nobody goes hungry, nobody is jobless or unprovided for, nobody needs to struggle for status. Vocational Apt determines a man's rightful place and function in society, and there's no longer the artificial distinction imposed by race, color or creed. War is a thing of the past. Best of all, the old-fashioned 'home-life,' with all of its unhealthy emotional ties, is being replaced by sensible conditioning when a child reaches school age. The umbilical cord is no longer a permanent leash, a strangler's noose, or a silver-plated life-line stretching back to the womb."

Harry Collins nodded. "I suppose only the exceptional cases ever need to go to a treatment center like this."

"Exactly."

"But what makes *me* one of the exceptions? Is it because of the way the folks brought me up, in a small town, with all the old-fashioned books and everything? Is that why I hated confinement and conformity so much? Is it because of all the years I spent reading? And why—"

Dr. Manschoff stood up. "You tempt me," he said. "You tempt me strongly. As you can see, I dearly love a lecture—and a captive audience. But right now, the audience must not remain captive. I prescribe an immediate dose of freedom."

"You mean I'm to leave here?"

"Is that what you want to do?"

"Frankly, no. Not if it means going back to my job."

"That hasn't been decided upon. We can discuss the problem later, and perhaps we can go into the answers to those questions you just posed. But at the moment, I'd suggest you stay with us, though without the restraint of remaining in your room or in the wards. In other words, I want you to start going outside again."

"Outside?"

"You'll find several square miles of open country just beyond the doors here. You're at liberty to wander around and enjoy yourself. Plenty of fresh air and sunshine—come and go as you wish. I've already issued instructions which permit you to keep your own hours. Meals will be available when you desire them."

"You're very kind."

"Nonsense. I'm prescribing what you need. And when the time comes, we'll arrange to talk again. You know where to find me."

Dr. Manschoff dismantled his steeple and placed a half of the roof in each trouser-pocket.

And Harry Collins went outdoors.

It was wonderful just to be free and alone—like returning to that faraway childhood in Wheaton once again. Harry appreciated every minute of it during the first week of his wandering.

But Harry wasn't a child any more, and after a week he began to wonder instead of wander.

The grounds around the treatment center were more than spacious; they seemed absolutely endless. No matter how far he walked during the course of a day, Harry had never encountered any walls, fences or artificial barriers; there was nothing to stay his progress but the natural barriers of high, steeply-slanting precipices which seemed to rim all sides of a vast valley. Apparently the center itself was set in the middle of a large canyon—a canyon big enough to contain an airstrip for helicopter landings. The single paved road leading from the main buildings terminated at the airstrip, and Harry saw helicopters arrive and depart from time to time; apparently they brought in food and supplies.

As for the center itself, it consisted of four large structures, two of which Harry was familiar with. The largest was made up of apartments for individual patients, and staffed by nurses and attendants. Harry's own room was here, on the second floor, and from the beginning he'd been allowed to roam around the communal halls below at will.

The second building was obviously administrative—Dr. Manschoff's private office was situated therein, and presumably the other staff-members operated out of here.

The other two buildings were apparently inaccessible; not guarded or policed or even distinguished by signs prohibiting access, but merely locked and unused. At least, Harry had found the doors locked when—out of normal curiosity—he had ventured to approach them. Nor had he ever seen anyone enter or leave the premises. Perhaps these structures were unnecessary under the present circumstances, and had been built for future accommodations.

Still, Harry couldn't help wondering.

And now, on this particular afternoon, he sat on the bank of the little river which ran through the valley, feeling the mid-summer sun beating down upon his forehead and staring down at the eddying current with its ripples and reflections.

Ripples and reflections....

Dr. Manschoff had answered his questions well, yet new questions had arisen.

Most people didn't go crazy any more, the doctor had explained, and so there were very few treatment centers such as this.

Question: Why were there any at all?

A place like this cost a fortune to staff and maintain. In an age where living-space and areable acreage was at such a premium, why waste this vast and fertile expanse? And in a society more and more openly committed to the policy of promoting the greatest good for the greatest number, why bother about the fate of an admittedly insignificant group of mentally disturbed patients?

Not that Harry resented his situation; in fact, it was almost too good to be true.

Question: Was it too good to be true?

Why, come to realize it, he'd seen less than a dozen other patients during his entire stay here! All of them were male, and all of them—apparently—were recovering from a condition somewhat similar to his own. At least, he'd recognized the same reticence and diffidence when it came to exchanging more than a perfunctory greeting in an encounter in an outer corridor. At the time, he'd accepted their unwillingness to communicate; welcomed and understood it because of *his* condition. And that in itself wasn't what he questioned now.

But why were there so *few* patients beside himself? Why were they all males? And why weren't *they* roaming the countryside now the way he was?

So many staff-members and so few patients. So much room and luxury and freedom, and so little use of it. So little apparent purpose to it all.

Question: Was there a hidden purpose?

Harry stared down into the ripples and reflections, and the sun was suddenly intolerably hot, its glare on the water suddenly blinding and bewildering. He saw his face mirrored on the water's surface, and it was not the familiar countenance he knew—the features were bloated, distorted, shimmering and wavering.

Maybe it was starting all over again. Maybe he was getting another one of those headaches. Maybe he was going to lose control again.

Yes, and maybe he was just imagining things. Sitting here in all this heat wasn't a good idea.

Why not take a swim?

That seemed reasonable enough. In fact, it seemed like a delightful distraction. Harry rose and stripped. He entered the water awkwardly—one didn't dive, not after twenty years of abstinence from the outdoor life—but he found that he could swim, after a fashion. The water was cooling, soothing. A few minutes of immersion and Harry found himself forgetting his speculations. The uneasy feeling had vanished. Now, when he stared down into the water, he saw his own face reflected, looking just the way it should. And when he stared up—

He saw her standing there, on the bank.

She was tall, slim, and blonde. Very tall, very slim, and very blonde.

She was also very desirable.

Up until a moment ago, Harry had considered swimming a delightful distraction. But now—

"How's the water?" she called.

"Fine."

She nodded, smiling down at him.

"Aren't you coming in?" he asked.

"No."

"Then what are you doing here?"

"I was looking for you, Harry."

"You know my name?"

She nodded again. "Dr. Manschoff told me."

"You mean, he sent you here to find me?"

"That's right."

"But I don't understand. If you're not going swimming, then why—I mean—"

Her smile broadened. "It's just part of the therapy, Harry."

"Part of the therapy?"

"That's right. *Part.*" She giggled. "Don't you think you'd like to come out of the water now and see what the rest of it might be?"

Harry thought so.

With mounting enthusiasm, he eagerly embraced his treatment and entered into a state of active cooperation.

It was some time before he ventured to comment on the situation. "Manschoff is a damned good diagnostician," he murmured. Then he sat up. "Are you a patient here?"

She shook her head. "Don't ask questions, Harry. Can't you be satisfied with things as they are?"

"You're just what the doctor ordered, all right." He gazed down at her. "But don't you even have a name?"

"You can call me Sue."

"Thank you."

He bent to kiss her but she avoided him and rose to her feet. "Got to go now."

"So soon?"

She nodded and moved towards the bushes above the bank.

"But when will I see you again?"

"Coming swimming tomorrow?"

"Yes."

"Maybe I can get away for more occupational therapy then."

She stooped behind the bushes, and Harry saw a flash of white.

"You *are* a nurse, aren't you," he muttered. "On the staff, I suppose. I should have known."

"All right, so I am. What's that got to do with it?"

"And I suppose you were telling the truth when you said Manschoff sent you here. This *is* just part of my therapy, isn't it?"

She nodded briefly as she slipped into her uniform. "Does that bother you, Harry?"

He bit his lip. When he spoke, his voice was low. "Yes, damn it, it does. I mean, I got the idea—at least, I was hoping—that this wasn't just a matter of carrying out an assignment on your part."

She looked up at him gravely. "Who said anything about an assignment, darling?" she murmured. "I volunteered."

And then she was gone.

Then she was gone, and then she came back that night in Harry's dreams, and then she was at the river the next day and it was better than the dreams, better than the day before.

Sue told him she had been watching him for weeks now. And she had gone to Manschoff and suggested it, and she was very glad. And they had to meet here, out in the open, so as not to complicate the situation or disturb any of the other patients.

So Harry naturally asked her about the other patients, and the whole general setup, and she said Dr. Manschoff would answer all those questions in due time. But right now, with only an hour or so to spare, was he going to spend it all asking for information? Matters were accordingly adjusted to their mutual satisfaction, and it was on that basis that they continued their almost daily meetings for some time.

The next few months were perhaps the happiest Harry had ever known. The whole interval took on a dreamlike quality—idealized, romanticized, yet basically sensual. There is probably such a dream buried deep within the psyche of every man, Harry reflected, but to few is it ever given to realize its reality. His early questioning attitude gave way to a mood of mere acceptance and enjoyment. This was the primitive drama, the very essence of the male-female relationship; Adam and Eve in the Garden. Why waste time seeking the Tree of Knowledge?

And it wasn't until summer passed that Harry even thought about the Serpent.

One afternoon, as he sat waiting for Sue on the river bank, he heard a sudden movement in the brush behind him.

"Darling?" he called, eagerly.

"Please, you don't know me *that* well." The deep masculine voice carried overtones of amusement.

Flushing, Harry turned to confront the intruder. He was a short, stocky, middle-aged man whose bristling gray crewcut almost matched the neutral shades of his gray orderly's uniform.

"Expecting someone else, were you?" the man muttered. "Well, I'll get out of your way."

"That's not necessary. I was really just daydreaming, I guess. I don't know what made me think—" Harry felt his flush deepen, and he lowered his eyes and his voice as he tried to improvise some excuse.

"You're a lousy liar," the man said, stepping forward and seating himself on the bank next to Harry. "But it doesn't really matter. I don't think your girl friend is going to show up today, anyway."

"What do you mean? What do you know about—"

"I mean just what I said," the man told him. "And I know everything I need to know, about you and about her and about the situation in general. That's why I'm here, Collins."

He paused, watching the play of emotions in Harry's eyes.

"I know what you're thinking right now," the gray-haired man continued. "At first you wondered how I knew your name. Then you realized that if I was on the staff in the wards I'd naturally be able to identify the patients. Now it occurs to you that you've never seen me in the wards, so you're speculating as to whether or not I'm working out of the administration offices with that psychiatric no good Manschoff. But if I were, I wouldn't be calling him names, would I? Which means you're really getting confused, aren't you, Collins? Good!"

The man chuckled, but there was neither mockery, malice, nor genuine mirth in the sound. And his eyes were sober, intent.

"Who are you?" Harry asked. "What are you doing here?"

"The name is Ritchie, Arnold Ritchie. At least, that's the name they know me by around here, and you can call me that. As to what I'm doing, it's a long story. Let's just say that right now I'm here to give you a little advanced therapy."

"Then Manschoff did send you?"

The chuckle came again, and Ritchie shook his head. "He did not. And if he even suspected I was here, there'd be hell to pay."

"Then what do you want with me?"

"It isn't a question of what I want. It's a question of what *you need.* Which is, like I said, advanced therapy. The sort that dear old kindly permissive Father-Image Manschoff doesn't intend you to get."

Harry stood up. "What's this all about?"

Ritchie rose with him, smiling for the first time. "I'm glad you asked that question, Collins. It's about time you did, you know. Everything has been so carefully planned to keep you from asking it. But you *were* beginning to wonder just a bit anyway, weren't you?"

"I don't see what you're driving at."

"You don't see what anyone is driving at, Collins. You've been blinded by a spectacular display of kindness, misdirected by self-indulgence. I told you I knew everything I needed to know about you, and I do. Now I'm going to ask you to remember these things for yourself; the things you've avoided considering all this while.

"I'm going to ask you to remember that you're twenty-eight years old, and that for almost seven years you were an agency man and a good one. You worked hard, you did a conscientious job, you stayed in line, obeyed the rules, never rebelled. Am I correct in my summary of the situation?"

"Yes, I guess so."

"So what was your reward for all this unceasing effort and eternal conformity? A one-room apartment and a one-week vacation, once a year. Count your blessings, Collins. Am I right?"

"Right."

"Then what happened? Finally you flipped, didn't you? Tried to take a header out of the window. You chucked your job, chucked your responsibilities, chucked your future and attempted to chuck yourself away. Am I still right?"

"Yes."

"Good enough. And now we come to the interesting part of the story. Seven years of being a good little boy got you nothing but the promise of present and future frustration. Seven seconds of madness, of attempted self-destruction, brought you here. And as a reward for bucking the system, the system itself has provided you with a life of luxury and leisure—full permission to come and go as you please, live in spacious ease, indulge in the gratification of every appetite, free of responsibility or restraint. Is that true?"

"I suppose so."

"All right. Now, let me ask you the question you asked me. What's it all about?"

Ritchie put his hand on Harry's shoulder. "Tell me that, Collins. Why do you suppose you've received such treatment? As long as you stayed in line, nobody gave a damn for your comfort or welfare. Then, when you committed the cardinal sin of our present-day society—when you rebelled—everything was handed to you on a silver platter. Does that make sense?"

"But it's therapy. Dr. Manschoff said—"

"Look, Collins. Millions of people flip every year. Millions more attempt suicide. How many of them end up in a place like this?"

"They don't, though. That's just Naturalist propaganda. Dr. Manschoff said—"

"*Dr. Manschoff said!* I know what he said, all right. And you believed him, because you wanted to believe him. You wanted the reassurance he could offer you—the feeling of being unique and important. So you didn't ask him any questions, you didn't ask any questions of yourself. Such as why anybody would consider an insignificant little agency man, without friends, family or connections, worth the trouble of rehabilitating at all, let alone amidst such elaborate and expensive surroundings. Why, men like you are a dime a dozen these days—Vocational Apt can push a few buttons and come up with half a million replacements to take over your job. You aren't important to society, Collins. You aren't important to anyone at all, besides yourself. And yet you got the red-carpet treatment. It's about time somebody yanked that carpet out from under you. What's it all about?"

Harry blinked. "Look here, I don't see why this is any of your business. Besides, to tell the truth, I'm expecting—"

"I know who you're expecting, but I've already told you she won't be here. Because she's expecting."

"What—?"

"It's high time you learned the facts of life, Collins. Yes, the well-known facts of life—the ones about the birds and the bees, and barefoot boys and blondes, too. Your little friend Sue is going to have a souvenir."

"I don't believe it! I'm going to ask Dr. Manschoff."

"Sure you are. You'll ask Manschoff and he'll deny it. And so you'll tell him about me. You'll say you met somebody in the woods today—either a lunatic or a Naturalist spy who infiltrated here under false pretenses. And Manschoff will reassure you. He'll reassure you just long enough to get his hands on me. Then he'll take care of both of us."

"Are you insinuating—"

"Hell, no! I'm *telling* you!" Ritchie put his hand down suddenly, and his voice calmed. "Ever wonder about those other two big buildings on the premises here, Collins? Well, I can tell you about one of them, because that's where I work. You might call it an experimental laboratory if you like. Sometime later on I'll describe it to you. But right now it's the other building that's important; the building with the big chimney. That's a kind of an incinerator, Collins—a place where the mistakes go up in smoke, at night, when there's nobody to see. A place where you and I will go up in smoke, if you're fool enough to tell Manschoff about this."

"You're lying."

"I wish to God I was, for both our sakes! But I can prove what I'm saying. *You* can prove it, for yourself."

"How?"

"Pretend this meeting never occurred. Pretend that you just spent the afternoon here, waiting for a girl who never showed up. Then do exactly what you would do under those circumstances. Go in to see Dr. Manschoff and ask him where Sue is, tell him you were worried because she'd promised to meet you and then didn't appear.

"I can tell you right now what he'll tell you. He'll say that Sue has been transferred to another treatment center, that she knew about it for several weeks but didn't want to upset you with the news of her departure. So she decided to just slip away. And Manschoff will tell you not to be unhappy. It just so happens that he knows of another nurse who has had her eye on you—a very pretty little brunette named Myrna. In fact, if you go down to the river tomorrow, you'll find her waiting for you there."

"What if I refuse?"

Ritchie shrugged. "Why should you refuse? It's all fun and games, isn't it? Up to now you haven't asked any questions about what was going on, and it would look very strange if you started at this late date. I strongly advise you to cooperate. If not, everything is likely to—quite literally—go up in smoke."

Harry Collins frowned. "All right, suppose I do what you say, and Manschoff gives me the answers you predict. This still doesn't prove that he'd be lying or that you're telling me the truth."

"Wouldn't it indicate as much, though?"

"Perhaps. But on the other hand, it could merely mean that you know Sue *has* been transferred, and that Dr. Manschoff intends to turn me over to a substitute. It doesn't necessarily imply anything sinister."

"In other words, you're insisting on a clincher, is that it?"

"Yes."

"All right." Ritchie sighed heavily. "You asked for it." He reached into the left-hand upper pocket of the gray uniform and brought out a small, stiff square of glossy paper.

"What's that?" Harry asked. He reached for the paper, but Ritchie drew his hand back.

"Look at it over my shoulder," he said. "I don't want any fingerprints. Hell of a risky business just smuggling it out of the files—no telling how well they check up on this material."

Harry circled behind the smaller man. He squinted down. "Hard to read."

"Sure. It's a photostat. I made it myself, this morning; that's my department. Read carefully now. You'll see it's a transcript of the lab report. Susan Pulver, that's her name, isn't it? After due examination and upon completion of preliminary tests, hereby found to be in the second month of pregnancy. Putative father, Harry Collins—that's you, see your name? And here's the rest of the record."

"Yes, let me see it. What's all this about inoculation series? And who is this Dr. Leffingwell?" Harry bent closer, but Ritchie closed his hand around the photostat and pocketed it again.

"Never mind that, now. I'll tell you later. The important thing is, do you believe me?"

"I believe Sue is pregnant, yes."

"That's enough. Enough for you to do what I've asked you to. Go to Manschoff and make inquiries. See what he tells you. Don't make a scene, and for God's sake don't mention my name. Just confirm my story for yourself. Then I'll give you further details."

"But when will I see you?"

"Tomorrow afternoon, if you like. Right here."

"You said he'd be sending another girl—"

Ritchie nodded. "So I did. And so he'll say. I suggest you beg to be excused for the moment. Tell him it will take a while for you to get over the shock of losing Sue this way."

"I won't be lying," Harry murmured.

"I know. And I'm sorry. Believe me, I am." Ritchie sighed again. "But you'll just have to trust me from now on."

"Trust you? When you haven't even explained what this is all about?"

"You've had your shock-therapy for today. Come back for another treatment tomorrow."

And then Ritchie was gone, the gray uniform melting away into the gray shadows of the shrubbery above the bank.

A short time later, Harry made his own way back to the center in the gathering twilight. The dusk was gray, too. Everything seemed gray now.

So was Harry Collins' face, when he emerged from his interview with Dr. Manschoff that evening. And it was still pallid the next afternoon when he came down to the river bank and waited for Ritchie to reappear.

The little man emerged from the bushes. He stared at Harry's drawn countenance and nodded slowly.

"I was right, eh?" he muttered.

"It looks that way. But I can't understand what's going on. If this isn't just a treatment center, if they're not really interested in my welfare, then what am I doing here?"

"You're taking part in an experiment. This, my friend, is a laboratory. And you are a nice, healthy guinea pig."

"But that doesn't make sense. I haven't been experimented on. They've let me do as I please."

"Exactly. And what do guinea pigs excel at? *Breeding.*"

"You mean this whole thing was rigged up just so that Sue and I would—?"

"Please, let's not be so egocentric, shall we? After all, you're not the *only* male patient in this place. There are a dozen others wandering around loose. Some of them have their favorite caves, others have discovered little bypaths, but all of them seem to have located ideal trysting-places. Whereupon, of course, the volunteer nurses have located *them*."

"Are you telling me the same situation exists with each of the others?"

"Isn't it fairly obvious? You've shown no inclination to become friendly with the rest of the patients here, and none of them have made any overtures to you. That's because everyone has his own little secret, his own private arrangement. And so all of you go around fooling everybody else, and all of you are being fooled. I'll give credit to Manschoff and his staff on that point—he's certainly mastered the principles of practical psychology."

"But you talked about breeding. With our present overpopulation problem, why in the world do they deliberately encourage the birth of more children?"

"Very well put. 'Why in the world' indeed! In order to answer that, you'd better take a good look at the world."

Arnold Ritchie seated himself on the grass, pulled out a pipe, and then replaced it hastily. "Better not smoke," he murmured. "Be awkward if we attracted any attention and were found together."

Harry stared at him. "You *are* a Naturalist, aren't you?"

"I'm a reporter, by profession."

"Which network?"

"No network. *Newzines*. There are still a few in print, you know."

"I know. But I can't afford them."

"There aren't many left who can, or who even feel the need of reading them. Nevertheless, mavericks like myself still cling to the ancient and honorable practices of the Fourth Estate. One of which is ferreting out the inside story, the news behind the news."

"Then you're not working for the Naturalists."

"Of course I am. I'm working for them and for everybody else who has an interest in learning the truth." Ritchie paused. "By the way, you keep using that term as if it were some kind of dirty word. Just what does it mean? What *is* a Naturalist, in your book?"

"Why, a radical thinker, of course. An opponent of government policies, of progress. One who believes we're running out of living space, using up the last of our natural resources."

"What do you suppose motivates Naturalists, really?"

"Well, they can't stand the pressures of daily living, or the prospects of a future when we'll be still more hemmed in."

Ritchie nodded. "Any more than you could, a few months ago, when you tried to commit suicide. Wouldn't you say that *you* were thinking like a Naturalist then?"

Harry grimaced. "I suppose so."

"Don't feel ashamed. You saw the situation clearly, just as the so-called Naturalists do. And just as the government does. Only the government can't dare admit it—hence the secrecy behind this project."

"A hush-hush government plan to stimulate further breeding? I still don't see—"

"Look at the world," Ritchie repeated. "Look at it realistically. What's the situation at present? Population close to six billion, and rising fast. There was a leveling-off period in the Sixties, and then it started to climb again. No wars, no disease to cut it down. The development of synthetic foods, the use of algae and fungi, rules out famine as a limiting factor. Increased harnessing of atomic power has done away with widespread poverty, so there's no economic deterrent to propagation. Neither church nor state dares set up a legal prohibition. So here we are, at the millennium. In place of international tension we've substituted internal tension. In place of thermonuclear explosion, we have a population explosion."

"You make it look pretty grim."

"I'm just talking about today. What happens ten years from now, when we hit a population-level of ten billion? What happens when we reach twenty billion, fifty billion, a hundred? Don't talk to me about more substitutes, more synthetics, new ways of conserving top-soil. There just isn't going to be *room* for everyone!"

"Then what's the answer?"

"That's what the government wants to know. Believe me, they've done a lot of searching; most of it *sub rosa*. And then along came this man Leffingwell, with *his* solution. That's just what it is, of course—an endocrinological solution, for direct injection."

"Leffingwell? The Dr. Leffingwell whose name was on that photostat? What's he got to do with all this?"

"He's boss of this project," Ritchie said. "He's the one who persuaded them to set up a breeding-center. You're *his* guinea pig."

"But why all the secrecy?"

"That's what I wanted to know. That's why I scurried around, pulled strings to get a lab technician's job here. It wasn't easy, believe me. The whole deal is being kept strictly under wraps until Leffingwell's experiments prove out. They realized right away that it would be fatal to use volunteers for the experiments—they'd be bound to talk, there'd be leaks. And of course, they anticipated some awkward results at first, until the technique is refined and perfected. Well, they were right on that score. I've seen some of their failures." Ritchie shuddered. "Any volunteer—any military man, government employee or even a so-called dedicated scientist who broke away would spread enough rumors about what was going on to kill the entire project. That's why they decided to use mental patients for subjects. God knows, they had millions to choose from, but they were very particular. You're a rare specimen, Collins."

"How so?"

"Because you happen to fit all their specifications. You're young, in good physical condition. Unlike ninety percent of the population, you don't even wear contact lenses, do you? And your aberration was temporary, easily removed by removing you from the tension-sources which created it. You have no family ties, no close friends, to question your absence. That's why you were chosen—one of the two hundred."

"Two hundred? But there's only a dozen others here now."

"A dozen males, yes. You're forgetting the females. Must be about fifty or sixty in the other building."

"But if you're talking about someone like Sue, she's a nurse—"

Ritchie shook his head. "That's what she was *told* to say. Actually, she's a patient, too. They're all patients. Twelve men and sixty women, at the moment. Originally, about thirty men and a hundred and seventy women."

"What happened to the others?"

"I told you there were some failures. Many of the women died in childbirth. Some of them survived, but found out about the results—and the results, up until now, haven't been perfect. A few of the men found out, too. Well, they have only one method of dealing with failures here. They dispose of them. I told you about that chimney, didn't I?"

"You mean they killed the offspring, killed those who found out about them?"

Ritchie shrugged.

"But what are they actually *doing*? Who is this Dr. Leffingwell? What's it all about?"

"I think I can answer those questions for you."

Harry wheeled at the sound of the familiar voice.

Dr. Manschoff beamed down at him from the top of the river bank. "Don't be alarmed," he said. "I wasn't following you with any intent to eavesdrop. I was merely concerned about him." His eyes flickered as he directed his gaze past Harry's shoulder, and Harry turned again to look at Arnold Ritchie.

The little man was no longer standing and he was no longer alone. Two attendants now supported him, one on either side, and Ritchie himself sagged against their grip with eyes closed. A hypodermic needle in one attendant's hand indicated the reason for Ritchie's sudden collapse.

"Merely a heavy sedative," Dr. Manschoff murmured. "We came prepared, in expectation of just such an emergency." He nodded at his companions. "Better take him back now," he said. "I'll look in on him this evening, when he comes out of it."

"Sorry about all this," Manschoff continued, sitting down next to Harry as the orderlies lifted Ritchie's inert form and carried him up the slanting slope. "It's entirely my fault. I misjudged my patient—never should have permitted him such a degree of freedom. Obviously, he's not ready for it yet. I do hope he didn't upset you in any way."

"No. He seemed quite"—Harry hesitated, then went on hastily—"logical."

"Indeed he is." Dr. Manschoff smiled. "Paranoid delusions, as they used to call them, can often be rationalized most convincingly. And from what little I heard, he was doing an excellent job, wasn't he?"

"Well—"

"I know." A slight sigh erased the smile. "Leffingwell and I are mad scientists, conducting biological experiments on human guinea pigs. We've assembled patients for breeding purposes and the government is secretly subsidizing us. Also, we incinerate our victims—again, with full governmental permission. All very logical, isn't it?"

"I didn't mean that," Harry told him. "It's just that he said Sue was pregnant and he was hinting things."

"Said?" Manschoff stood up. "*Hinted?* I'm surprised he didn't go further than that. Just today, we discovered he'd been using the office facilities—he had a sort of probationary position, as you may have guessed, helping out the staff in administration—to provide tangible proof of his artistic creations. He was writing out 'official reports' and then photostating them. Apparently he intended to circulate the results as 'evidence' to support his delusions. Look, here's a sample."

Dr. Manschoff passed a square of glossy paper to Harry, who scanned it quickly. It was another laboratory report similar to the one Ritchie had shown him, but containing a different set of names.

"No telling how long this sort of thing has been going on," Manschoff said. "He may have made dozens. Naturally, the moment we discovered it, we realized prompt action was necessary. He'll need special attention."

"But what's wrong with him?"

"It's a long story. He was a reporter at one time—he may have told you that. The death of his wife precipitated a severe trauma and brought him to our attention. Actually, I'm not at liberty to say any more regarding his case; you understand, I'm sure."

"Then you're telling me that everything he had to say was a product of his imagination?"

"No, don't misunderstand. It would be more correct to state that he merely distorted reality. For example, there *is* a Dr. Leffingwell on the staff here; he is a diagnostician and has nothing to do with psychotherapy *per se.* And he has charge of the hospital ward in Unit Three, the third building you may have noticed behind Administration. That's where the nurses maintain residence, of course. Incidentally, when any nurses take on a—special assignment, as it were, such as yours, Leffingwell does examine and treat them. There's a new oral contraception technique he's evolved which may be quite efficacious. But I'd hardly call it an example of sinister experimentation under the circumstances, would you?"

Harry shook his head. "About Ritchie, though," he said. "What will happen to him?"

"I can't offer any prognosis. In view of my recent error in judgment concerning him, it's hard to say how he'll respond to further treatment. But rest assured that I'll do my best for his case. Chances are you'll be seeing him again before very long."

Dr. Manschoff glanced at his watch. "Shall we go back now?" he suggested. "Supper will be served soon."

The two men toiled up the bank.

Harry discovered that the doctor was right about supper. It was being served as he returned to his room. But the predictions concerning Ritchie didn't work out quite as well.

It was after supper—indeed, quite some hours afterwards, while Harry sat at his window and stared sleeplessly out into the night—that he noted the thick, greasy spirals of black smoke rising suddenly from the chimney of the Third Unit building. And the sight may have prepared him for the failure of Dr. Manschoff's prophecy regarding his disturbed patient.

Harry never asked any questions, and no explanations were ever forthcoming.

But from that evening onward, nobody ever saw Arnold Ritchie again.

3. President Winthrop—1999

The Secretary of State closed the door.

"Well?" he asked.

President Winthrop looked up from the desk and blinked. "Hello, Art," he said. "Sit down."

"Sorry I'm late," the Secretary told him. "I came as soon as I got the call."

"It doesn't matter." The President lit a cigarette and pursed his lips around it until it stopped wobbling. "I've been checking the reports all night."

"You look tired."

"I am. I could sleep for a week. That is, I *wish* I could."

"Any luck?"

The President pushed the papers aside and drummed the desk for a moment. Then he offered the Secretary a gray ghost of a smile.

"The answer's still the same."

"But this was our last chance—"

"I know." The President leaned back. "When I think of the time and effort, the money that's been poured into these projects! To say nothing of the hopes we had. And now, it's all for nothing."

"You can't say that," the Secretary answered. "After all, we did reach the moon. We got to Mars." He paused. "No one can take that away from you. You sponsored the Martian flights. You fought for the appropriations, pushed the project, carried it through. You helped mankind realize its greatest dream—"

"Save that for the newscasts," the President said. "The fact remains, we've succeeded. And our success was a failure. Mankind's greatest dream, eh? Read these reports and you'll find out this is mankind's greatest nightmare."

"Is it that bad?"

"Yes." The President slumped in his chair. "It's that bad. We can reach the moon at will. Now we can send a manned flight to Mars. But it means nothing. We can't support life in either place. There's absolutely no possibility of establishing or maintaining an outpost, let alone a large colony or a permanent human residence. That's what all the reports conclusively demonstrate.

"Every bit of oxygen, every bit of food and clothing and material, would have to be supplied. And investigations prove there's no chance of ever realizing any return. The cost of such an operation is staggeringly prohibitive. Even if there was evidence to show it might be possible to undertake some mining projects, it wouldn't begin to defray expenses, once you consider the transportation factor."

"But if they improve the rockets, manage to make room for a bigger payload, wouldn't it be cheaper?"

"It would still cost roughly a billion dollars to equip a flight and maintain a personnel of twenty men for a year," the President told him. "I've checked into that, and even this estimate is based on the most optimistic projection. So you can see there's no use in continuing now. We'll never solve our problems by attempting to colonize the moon or Mars."

"But it's the only possible solution left to us."

"No it isn't," the President said. "There's always our friend Leffingwell."

The Secretary of State turned away. "You can't officially sponsor a thing like that," he muttered. "It's political suicide."

The gray smile returned to the gray lips. "Suicide? What do you know about suicide, Art? I've been reading a few statistics on *that*, too. How many actual suicides do you think we had in this country last year?"

"A hundred thousand? Two hundred, maybe?"

"Two million." The President leaned forward. "Add to that, over a million murders and six million crimes of violence."

"I never knew—"

"Damned right you didn't! We used to have a Federal Bureau of Investigation to help prevent such things. Now the big job is merely to hush them up. We're doing everything in our power just to keep these matters quiet, or else there'd be utter panic. Then there's the accident total and the psycho rate. We can't build institutions fast enough to hold the mental cases, nor train doctors enough to care for them. Shifting them into other jobs in other areas doesn't cure, and it no longer even disguises what is happening. At this rate, another ten years will see half the nation going insane. And it's like this all over the world.

"This is race-suicide, Art. Race-suicide through sheer fecundity. Leffingwell is right. The reproductive instinct, unchecked, will overbalance group survival in the end. How long has it been since you were out on the streets?"

The Secretary of State shrugged. "You know I never go out on the streets," he said. "It isn't very safe."

"Of course not. But it's no safer for the hundreds of millions who have to go out every day. Accident, crime, the sheer maddening proximity of the crowds—these phenomena are increasing through mathematical progression. And they must be stopped. Leffingwell has the only answer."

"They won't buy it," warned the Secretary. "Congress won't, and the voters won't, any more than they bought birth-control. And this is worse."

"I know that, too." The President rose and walked over to the window, looking out at the sky-scraper apartments which loomed across what had once been the Mall. He was trying to find the dwarfed spire of Washington's Monument in the tangled maze of stone.

"If I go before the people and sponsor Leffingwell, I'm through. Through as President, through with the Party. They'll crucify me. But somebody in authority must push this project. That's the beginning. Once it's known, people will have to think about the possibilities. There'll be opposition, then controversy, then debate. And gradually Leffingwell will gain adherents. It may take five years, it may take ten. Finally, the change will come. First through volunteers. Then by law. I only pray that it happens soon."

"They'll curse your name," the Secretary said. "They'll try to kill you. It's going to be hell."

"Hell for me if I do, yes. Worse hell for the whole world if I don't."

"But are you quite sure it will work? His method, I mean?"

"You saw the reports on his tests, didn't you? It works, all right. We've got more than just abstract data, now. We've got films for the telescreenings all set up."

"Films? You mean you'll actually *show* what the results are? Why, just telling the people will be bad enough. And admitting the government sponsored the project under wraps. But when they *see*, nothing on earth can save you from assassination."

"Perhaps. It doesn't really matter." The President crushed his cigarette in the ashtray. "One less mouth to feed. And I'm getting pretty sick of synthetic meals, anyway."

President Winthrop turned to the Secretary, his eyes brightening momentarily. "Tell you what, Art. I'm not planning on breaking the proposal to the public until next Monday. What say we have a little private dinner party on Saturday evening, just the Cabinet members and their wives? Sort of a farewell celebration, in a way, but we won't call it that, of course? Chef tells me there's still twenty pounds of hamburger in the freezers."

"Twenty pounds of hamburger? You mean it?" The Secretary of State was smiling, too.

"That's right." The President of the United States grinned in anticipation. "Been a long time since I've tasted a real, honest-to-goodness hamburger."

4. Harry Collins—2000

Harry didn't ask any questions. He just kept his mouth shut and waited. Maybe Dr. Manschoff suspected and maybe he didn't. Anyway, there was no trouble. Harry figured there wouldn't be, as long as he stayed in line and went through the proper motions. It was all a matter of pretending to conform, pretending to agree, pretending to believe.

So he watched his step—*except in the dreams, and then he was always falling into the yawning abyss.*

He kept his nose clean—*but in the dreams he smelled the blood and brimstone of the pit.*

He managed to retain a cheerful smile at all times—*though, in the dreams, he screamed.*

Eventually, he even met Myrna. She was the pretty little brunette whom Ritchie had mentioned, and she did her best to console him—*only in dreams, when he embraced her, he was embracing a writhing coil of slimy smoke.*

It may have been that Harry Collins went a little mad, just having to pretend that he was sane. But he learned the way, and he managed. He saved the madness (*or was it the reality?*) for the dreams.

Meanwhile he waited and said nothing.

He said nothing when, after three months or so, Myrna was suddenly "transferred" without warning.

He said nothing when, once a week or so, he went in to visit with Dr. Manschoff.

He said nothing when Manschoff volunteered the information that Ritchie had been "transferred" too, or suggested that it would be best to stay on for "further therapy."

And he said nothing when still a third nurse came his way; a woman who was callid, complaisant, and nauseatingly nymphomaniac.

The important thing was to stay alive. Stay alive and try to learn.

It took him almost an additional year to find out what he wanted to find out. More than eight months passed before he found a way of sneaking out of his room at night, and a way of getting into that Third Unit through a delivery door which was occasionally left open through negligence.

Even then, all he learned was that the female patients did have their living quarters here, along with the members of the staff and—presumably—Dr. Leffingwell. Many of the women *were* patients rather than nurses, as claimed, and a good number of them were in various stages of pregnancy, but this proved nothing.

Several times Harry debated the possibilities of taking some of the other men in his Unit into his confidence. Then he remembered what had happened to Arnold Ritchie and decided against this course. The risk was too great. He had to continue alone.

It wasn't until Harry managed to get into Unit Four that he got what he wanted (what he *didn't* want) and learned that reality and dreams were one and the same.

There was the night, more than a year after he'd come to the treatment center, when he finally broke into the basement and found the incinerators. And the incinerators led to the operating and delivery chambers, and the delivery chambers led to the laboratory and the laboratory led to the incubators and the incubators led to the nightmare.

In the nightmare Harry found himself looking down at the mistakes and the failures and he recognized them for what they were, and he knew then why the incinerators were kept busy and why the black smoke poured.

In the nightmare he saw the special units containing those which were not mistakes or failures, and in a way they were worse than the others. They were red and wriggling there beneath the glass, and on the glass surfaces hung the charts which gave the data. Then Harry saw the names, saw his own name repeated twice—once for Sue, once for Myrna. And he realized that he had contributed to the successful outcome or issue of the experiments (*outcome? Issue? These horrors?*) and that was why Manschoff must have chosen to take the risk of keeping him alive. Because he was one of the *good* guinea pigs, and he had spawned, spawned living, mewing abominations.

He had dreamed of these things, and now he saw that they were real, so that nightmare merged with *now*, and he could gaze down at it with open eyes and scream at last with open mouth.

Then, of course, an attendant came running (*although he seemed to be moving ever so slowly, because everything moves so slowly in a dream*) and Harry saw him coming and lifted a bell-glass and smashed it down over the man's head (*slowly, ever so slowly*) and then he heard the others coming and he climbed out of the window and ran.

The searchlights winked across the courtyards and the sirens vomited hysteria from metallic throats and the night was filled with shadows that pursued.

But Harry knew where to run. He ran straight through the nightmare, through all the fantastic but familiar convolutions of sight and sound, and then he came to the river and plunged in.

Now the nightmare was not sight or sound, but merely sensation. Icy cold and distilled darkness; ripples that ran, then raced and roiled and roared. But there had to be a way out of the nightmare and there had to be a way out of the canyon, and that way was the river.

Apparently no one else had thought of the river; perhaps they had considered it as a possible avenue of escape and then discarded the notion when they realized how it ripped and raged among the rocks as it finally plunged from the canyon's mouth. Obviously, no one could hope to combat that current and survive.

But strange things happen in nightmares. And you fight the numbness and the blackness and you claw and convulse and you twist and turn and toss and then you ride the crests of frenzy and plunge into the troughs of panic and despair and you sweep round and round and sink down into nothingness until you break through to the freedom which comes only with oblivion.

Somewhere beyond the canyon's moiling maw, Harry Collins found that freedom and that oblivion. He escaped from the nightmare, just as he escaped from the river.

The river itself roared on without him.

And the nightmare continued, too....

5. Minnie Schultz—2009

When Frank came home, Minnie met him at the door. She didn't say a word, just handed him the envelope containing the notice.

"What's the matter?" Frank asked, trying to take her in his arms. "You been crying."

"Never mind." Minnie freed herself. "Just read what it says there."

Frank read slowly, determinedly, his features contorted in concentration. Vocational Apt had terminated his schooling at the old grade-school level, and while like all students he had been taught enough so that he could read the necessary advertising commercials, any printed message of this sort provided a definite challenge.

Halfway through the notice he started to scowl. "What kind of monkey business is this?"

"No monkey business. It's the new law. Everybody that gets married in Angelisco takes the shots, from now on. Fella from State Hall, he told me when he delivered this."

"We'll see about this," Frank muttered. "No damn government's gonna tell me how to run my life. Sa free country, ain't so?"

Minnie's mouth began to twitch. "They're coming back tomorra morning, the fella said. To give me the first shots. Gee, honey, I'm scared, like. I don't want 'em."

"That settles it," Frank said. "We're getting out of this place, fast."

"Where'd we go?"

"Dunno. Someplace. Texas, maybe. I was listening to the 'casts at work today. They don't have this law in Texas. Not yet, anyway. Come on, start packing."

"Packing? But how'll we get there?"

"Fly. We'll jet right out."

"You got prior'ty reservations or something?"

"No." The scowl returned to Frank's forehead. "But maybe if I pitch 'em a sob story, tell 'em it's our honeymoon, you know, then we could—"

Minnie shook her head. "It won't work, honey. You know that. Takes six months to get a prior'ty clearance or whatever they call it. Besides, your job and all—what'll you do in Texas? They've got your number listed here. Why, we couldn't even *land*, like. I bet Texas is even more crowded than Angelisco these days, in the cities. And all the rest of it is Ag Culture project, isn't it?"

Frank was leaning against the sink, listening. Now he took three steps forward and sat down on the bed. He didn't look at her as he spoke.

"Well, we gotta do something," he said. "You don't want those shots and that's for sure. Maybe I can have one of those other things instead, those whaddya-call-'ems."

"You mean where they operate you, like?"

"That's right. A vas-something. You know, sterilize you. Then we won't have to worry."

Minnie took a deep breath. Then she sat down and put her arm around Frank.

"But you wanted kids," she murmured. "You told me, when we got married, you always wanted to have a son—"

Frank pulled away.

"Sure I do," he said. "A son. That's what I want. A *real* son. Not a freak. Not a damned little monster that has to go to the Clinic every month and take injections so it won't grow. And what happens to you if you take *your* shots now? What if they drive you crazy or something?"

Minnie put her arm around Frank again and made him look at her. "That's not true," she told him. "That's just a lot of Naturalist talk. I know."

"Hell you do."

"But I do, honey! Honest, like! May Stebbins, she took the shots last year, when they asked for volunteers. And she's all right. You seen her baby yourself, remember? It's the sweetest little thing, and awful smart! So maybe it wouldn't be so bad."

"I'll ask about being operated tomorrow," Frank said. "Forget it. It don't matter."

"Of course it matters." Minnie looked straight at him. "Don't you think I know what you been going through? Sweating it out on that job day after day, going nuts in the traffic, saving up the ration coupons so's we'd have extra food for the honeymoon and all?

"You didn't have to marry me, you know that. It was just like we could have a place of our own together, and kids. Well, we're gonna have 'em, honey. I'll take the shots."

Frank shook his head but said nothing.

"It won't be so bad," Minnie went on. "The shots don't hurt at all, and they make it easier, carrying the baby. They say you don't even get morning sickness or anything. And just think, when we have a kid, we get a chance for a bigger place. We go right on the housing lists. We can have two rooms. A real bedroom, maybe."

Frank stared at her. "Is that all you can think about?" he asked. "A real bedroom?"

"But honey—"

"What about the kid?" he muttered. "How you suppose it's gonna feel? How'd you like to grow up and *not* grow up? How'd you like to be a midget three feet high in a world where everybody else is bigger? What kind of a life you call *that*? I want my son to have a decent chance."

"He will have."

Minnie stared back at him, but she wasn't seeing his face. "Don't you understand, honey? This isn't just something happening to *us*. We're not special. It's happening to everybody, all over the country, all over the world. You seen it in the 'casts, haven't you? Most states, they adopted the laws. And in a couple more years it'll be the only way anyone will ever have kids. Ten, twenty years from now, the kids will be growing up. Ours won't be different then, because from now on all the kids will be just like he is. The same size."

"I thought you was afraid of the shots," Frank said.

Minnie was still staring. "I was, honey. Only, I dunno. I keep thinking about Grandma."

"What's the old lady got to do with it?"

"Well, I remember when I was a little girl, like. How my Grandma always used to tell me about *her* Grandma, when *she* was a little girl.

"She was saying about how in the old days, before there even was an Angelisco—when her Grandma came out here in a covered wagon. Just think, honey, she was younger than I am, and she come thousands and thousands of miles in a wagon! With real horses, like! Wasn't any houses, no people or nothing. Except Indians that shot at them. And they climbed up the mountains and they crossed over the deserts and went hungry and thirsty and had fights with those Indians all the way. But they never stopped until they got here. Because they was the pioneers."

"Pioneers?"

"That's what Grandma said *her* Grandma called herself. A pioneer. She was real proud of it, too. Because it means having the courage to cut loose from all the old things and try something new when you need to. Start a whole new world, a whole new kind of life."

She sighed. "I always wanted to be a pioneer, like, but I never thought I'd get the chance."

"What are you talking about? What's all this got to do with us, or having a kid?"

"Don't you see? Taking these shots, having a baby this new way—it's sort of being a pioneer, too. Gonna help bring a new kind of people into a new kind of world. And if that's not being a pioneer, like, it's the closest I can come to it. It sounds right to me now."

Minnie smiled and nodded. "I guess I made up my mind just now. I'm taking the shots."

"Hell you are!" Frank told her. "We'll talk about it some more in the morning."

But Minnie continued to smile.

And that night, as she lay in the utility bed, the squeaking of the springs became the sound of turning wheels. The plastic walls and ceiling of the eightieth-floor apartment turned to billowing canvas, and the thunder of the passing jets transformed itself into the drumming hoofbeats of a million buffalo.

Let Frank talk to her again in the morning if he liked, Minnie thought. *It wouldn't make any difference now. Because you can't stop us pioneers.*

---

6. Harry Collins—2012

Harry crouched behind the boulders, propping the rifle up between the rocks, and adjusted the telescopic sights. The distant doorway sprang into sharp focus. Grunting with satisfaction, he settled down to his vigil. The rifle-barrel had been dulled down against detection by reflection, and Harry's dark glasses protected him against the glare of the morning sun. He might have to wait several hours now, but he didn't care. It had taken him twelve years to come this far, and he was willing to wait a little while longer.

Twelve years. Was it really that long?

A mirror might have answered him; a mirror might have shown him the harsh features of a man of forty-two. But Harry needed no mirror. He could remember the past dozen years only too easily—though they had not been easy years.

Surviving the river was only the beginning. Animal strength carried him through that ordeal. But he emerged from the river as an animal; a wounded animal, crawling through the brush and arroyo outside the southern Colorado canyon.

And it was animal cunning which preserved him. He'd wandered several days until he encountered Emil Grizek and his outfit. By that time he was half-starved and completely delirious. It took a month until he was up and around again.

But Emil and the boys had nursed him through. They took turns caring for him in the bunkhouse; their methods were crude but efficient and Harry was grateful. Best of all, they asked no questions. Harry's status was that of a hunted fugitive, without a Vocational Apt record or rating. The authorities or any prospective employers would inquire into these things, but Emil Grizek never seemed curious. By the time Harry was up and around again, he'd been accepted as one of the bunch. He told them his name was Harry Sanders, and that was enough.

Two months after they found him, he'd signed on with Emil Grizek and found a new role in life.

Harry Collins, advertising copywriter, had become Harry Sanders, working cowhand.

There was surprisingly little difficulty. Grizek had absentee employers who weren't interested in their foreman's methods, just as long as he recruited his own wranglers for the Bar B Ranch. Nobody demanded to see Apt cards or insisted on making out formal work-reports, and the pay was in cash. Cowhands were hard to come by these days, and it was an unspoken premise that the men taking on such jobs would be vagrants, migratory workers, fugitives from justice and injustice. A generation or so ago they might have become tramps—but the last of the hoboes had vanished along with the last of the freight trains. Once the derelicts haunted the canyons of the big cities; today there was no place for them there, so they fled to the canyons of the west. Harry had found himself a new niche, and no questions asked.

Oddly enough, he fitted in. The outdoor life agreed with him, and in a matter of months he was a passable cowpoke; within a year he was one of Grizek's top hands.

He learned to ride a bucking jeep with the best of them, and he could spot, single out, and stun a steer in forty seconds flat; then use his electronic brander on it and have the critter back on its feet in just under a minute.

Work was no problem, and neither was recreation. The bunkhouse offered crude but adequate facilities for living; old-fashioned air-conditioning and an antique infra-red broiler seemed good enough for roughing it, and Cookie at least turned out real man-sized meals. Eating genuine beef and honest-to-goodness baked bread was a treat, and so was having the luxury of all that space in the sleeping quarters. Harry thrived on it.

And some of the other hands were interesting companions. True, they were renegades and mavericks, but they were each of them unique and individual, and Harry enjoyed listening to them fan the breeze during the long nights.

There was Big Phil, who was pushing sixty now. But you'd never know it, not unless you got him to talking about the old days when he'd been a boy in Detroit. His daddy had been one of the last of the Union Men, back in the days of what they used to call the Organized Labor Movement. He could tell you about wage-hour agreements and the Railroad Brotherhood and contract negotiations almost as if he knew of these things through personal experience. He even remembered the Democratic Party. Phil got out when the government took over and set up Vocational Apt and Industrial Supervision; that's when he drifted west.

Tom Lowery's family had been military; he claimed to have been a member of the last graduating class ever to leave West Point. When the armament race ended, his prospects of a career vanished, and he settled down as a guard at Canaveral. Finally, he'd headed for the open country.

Bassett was the scholar of the outfit. He could sit around and quote old-time book-authors by the hour—classic writers like Prather and Spillane. In another age he might have been a college professor or even a football coach; he had an aptitude for the arts.

And there was Lobo, the misogynist, who had fled a wife and eleven children back in Monterey; and Januzki, who used to be mixed up with one of those odd religious cults out on the Coast. He bragged he'd been one of the Big Daddy-Os in the Beat Generationists, and he argued with Bassett about some old-time evangelist named Kerouac.

Best of all, though, Harry liked talking to Nick Kendrick. Nick's hobby was music, and he treasured his second-hand stereophonic unit and collection of tapes. He too was a classicist in his way, and there was many a long winter night when Harry sat there listening to ancient folk songs. The quaint atonalities of progressive jazz and the childishly frantic rhythms of "cool sounds" were somehow soothing and reassuring in their reminder of a simple heritage from a simpler age.

But above all, these men were wranglers, and they took a peculiar pride in the traditions of their own calling. There wasn't a one of them who wouldn't spend hours mulling over the lore of the range and the prairie. They knew the Great Names from the Great Days—Eugene Autry, Wyatt Earp, the legendary Thomas Mix, Dale Robertson, Paladin, and all the others; men who rode actual horses in the era when the West was really an untamed frontier.

And like the cowboys they were, they maintained the customs of other days. Every few months they rode a bucking helicopter into some raw western town—Las Vegas, or Reno, or even over to Palm Springs—to drink recklessly in the cocktail lounges, gamble wildly at the slots, or "go down the line" with some telescreen model on location for outdoor ad-backgrounds. There were still half a dozen such sin-cities scattered throughout the west; even the government acknowledged the need of lonely men to blow off steam. And though Ag Culture officially disapproved of the whole cowhand system, and talked grimly of setting up new and more efficient methods for training personnel and handling the cattle ranges, nothing was ever done. Perhaps the authorities knew that it was a hopeless task; only the outcasts and iconoclasts had the temperament necessary to survive such loneliness under an open sky. City-dwelling conformists just could not endure the monotony.

But even Emil Grizek's hands marvelled at the way Harry lived. He never joined them in their disorderly descent upon the scarlet cities of the plain, and most of the time he didn't even seem to watch the telescreen. If anything, he deliberately avoided all possible contact with civilization.

Since he never volunteered any information about his own past, they privately concluded that he was just a psychopathic personality.

"Strong regressive and seclusive tendencies," Bassett explained, solemnly.

"Sure," Nick Kendrick nodded, wisely. "You mean a Mouldy Fig, like."

"Creeping Meatball," muttered cultist Januzki. Not being religious fanatics, the others didn't understand the reference. But gradually they came to accept Harry's isolationist ways as the norm—at least, for him. And since he never quarreled, never exhibited any signs of dissatisfaction, he was left to his own pattern.

Thus it was all the more surprising when that pattern was rudely and abruptly shattered.

Harry remembered the occasion well. It was the day the Leff Law was officially upheld by the Supremist Courts. The whole business came over the telescreens and there was no way of avoiding it—you couldn't avoid it, because everybody was talking about it and everybody was watching.

"Now what do you think?" Emil Grizek demanded. "Any woman wants a baby, she's got to have those shots. They say kids shrink down into nothing. Weigh less than two pounds when they're born, and never grow up to be any bigger than midgets. You ask me, the whole thing's plumb loco, to say nothing of psychotic."

"I dunno." This from Big Phil. "Reckon they just about have to do something, the way cities are filling up and all. Tell me every spot in the country, except for the plains states here, is busting at the seams. Same in Europe, Africa, South America. Running out of space, running out of food, all over the world. This man Leffingwell figures on cutting down on size so's to keep the whole shebang going."

"But why couldn't it be done on a voluntary basis?" Bassett demanded. "These arbitrary rulings are bound to result in frustrations. And can you imagine what will happen to the individual family constellations? Take a couple that already has two youngsters, as of now. Suppose the wife submits to the inoculations for her next child and it's born with a size-mutation. How in the world will that child survive as a midget in a family of giants? There'll be untold damage to the personality—"

"We've heard all those arguments," Tom Lowery cut in. "The Naturalists have been handing out that line for years. What happens to the new generation of kids, how do we know they won't be mentally defective, how can they adjust, by what right does the government interfere with private lives, personal religious beliefs; all that sort of thing. For over ten years now the debate's been going on. And meanwhile, time is running out. Space is running out. Food is running out. It isn't a question of individual choice any longer—it's a question of group survival. I say the Courts are right. We have to go according to law. And back the law up with force of arms if necessary."

"We get the message," Januzki agreed. "But something tells me there'll be trouble. Most folks need a midget like they need a monkey on their backs."

"It's a gasser, pardners," said Nick Kendrick. "Naturalists don't dig this. They'll fight it all along the line. Everybody's gonna be all shook up."

"It is still a good idea," Lobo insisted. "This Dr. Leffingwell, he has made the tests. For years he has given injections and no harm has come. The children are healthy, they survive. They learn in special schools—"

"How do you know?" Bassett demanded. "Maybe it's all a lot of motivationalist propaganda."

"We have seen them on the telescreens, no?"

"They could be faking the whole thing."

"But Leffingwell, he has offered the shots to other governments beside our own. The whole world will adopt them—"

"What if some countries don't? What if our kids become midgets and the Asiatics refuse the inoculations?"

"They won't. They need room even more than we do."

"No sense arguing," Emil Grizek concluded. "It's the law. You know that. And if you don't like it, join the Naturalists." He chuckled. "But better hurry. Something tells me there won't be any Naturalists around after a couple of years. Now that there's a Leff Law, the government isn't likely to stand for too much criticism." He turned to Harry. "What do you think?" he asked.

Harry shrugged. "No comment," he said.

But the next day he went to Grizek and demanded his pay in full.

"Leaving?" Grizek muttered. "I don't understand. You've been with us almost five years. Where you going, what you intend to do? What's got into you all of a sudden?"

"Time for a change," Harry told him. "I've been saving my money."

"Don't I know it? Never touched a penny in all this time." Grizek ran a hand across his chin. "Say, if it's a raise you're looking for, I can—"

"No, thanks. It's not that. I've money enough."

"So you have. Around eighteen, twenty thousand, I reckon, what with the bonuses." Emil Grizek sighed. "Well, if you insist, that's the way it's got to be, I suppose. When you plan on taking off?"

"Just as soon as there's a 'copter available."

"Got one going up to Colorado Springs tomorrow morning for the mail. I can get you aboard, give you a check—"

"I'll want my money in cash."

"Well, now, that isn't so easy. Have to send up for a special draft. Take a week or so."

"I can wait."

"All right. And think it over. Maybe you'll decide to change your mind."

But Harry didn't change his mind. And ten days later he rode a 'copter into town, his money-belt strapped beneath his safety-belt.

From Colorado Springs he jetted to Kancity, and from Kancity to Memphisee. As long as he had money, nobody asked any questions. He holed up in cheap airtels and waited for developments.

It wasn't easy to accustom himself to urbanization again. He had been away from cities for over seven years now, and it might well have been seven centuries. The overpopulation problem was appalling. The outlawing of private automotive vehicles had helped, and the clearing of the airlanes served a purpose; the widespread increase in the use of atomic power cut the smog somewhat. But the synthetic food was frightful, the crowding intolerable, and the welter of rules and regulations attending the performance of even the simplest human activity past all his comprehension. Ration cards were in universal use for almost everything; fortunately for Harry, the black market accepted cash with no embarrassing inquiries. He found that he could survive.

But Harry's interest was not in survival; he was bent upon destruction. Surely the Naturalists would be organized and planning a way!

Back in '98, of course, they'd been merely an articulate minority without formal unity—an abstract, amorphous group akin to the "Liberals" of previous generations. A Naturalist could be a Catholic priest, a Unitarian layman, an atheist factory hand, a government employee, a housewife with strong prejudices against governmental controls, a wealthy man who deplored the dangers of growing industrialization, an Ag Culture worker who dreaded the dwindling of individual rights, an educator who feared widespread employment of social psychology, or almost anyone who opposed the concept of Mass Man, Mass-Motivated. Naturalists had never formed a single class, a single political party.

Surely, however, the enactment of the Leffingwell Law would have united them! Harry knew there was strong opposition, not only on the higher levels but amongst the general population. People would be afraid of the inoculations; theologians would condemn the process; economic interests, real-estate owners and transportation magnates and manufacturers would sense the threat here. They'd sponsor and they'd subsidize their spokesmen and the Naturalists would evolve into an efficient body of opposition.

So Harry hoped, and so he thought, until he came out into the cities; came out into the cities and realized that the very magnitude of Mass Man mitigated against any attempt to organize him, except as a creature who labored and consumed. Organization springs from discussion, and discussion from thought—but who can think in chaos, discuss in delirium, organize in a vacuum? And the common citizen, Harry realized, had seemingly lost the capacity for group action. He remembered his own existence years ago—either he was lost in a crowd or he was alone, at home. Firm friendships were rare, and family units survived on the flimsiest of foundations. It took too much time and effort just to follow the rules, follow the traffic, follow the incessant routines governing even the simplest life-pattern in the teeming cities. For leisure there was the telescreen and the yellowjackets, and serious problems could be referred to the psych in routine check-ups. Everybody seemed lost in the crowd these days.

Harry discovered that Dr. Manschoff had indeed lied to him; mental disorders were on the increase. He remembered an old, old book—one of the very first treatises on sociological psychology. *The Lonely Crowd*, wasn't it? Full of mumbo-jumbo about "inner-directed" and "outer-directed" personalities. Well, there was a grain of truth in it all. The crowd, and its individual members, lived in loneliness. And since you didn't know very many people well enough to talk to, intimately, you talked to yourself. Since you couldn't get away from physical contact with others whenever you ventured abroad, you stayed inside—except when you had to go to work, had to line up for food-rations or supplies, had to wait for hours for your check-ups on off-days. And staying inside meant being confined to the equivalent of an old-fashioned prison cell. If you weren't married, you lived in "solitary"; if you were married, you suffered the presence of fellow-inmates whose habits became intolerable, in time. So you watched the screen more and more, or you increased your quota of sedation, and when that didn't help you looked for a real escape. It was always available to you if you searched long enough; waiting at the tip of a knife, in the coil of a rope, the muzzle of a gun. You could find it at the very bottom of a bottle of pills or at the very bottom of the courtyard outside your window. Harry recalled looking for it there himself, so many years ago.

But now he was looking for something else. He was looking for others who shared not only his viewpoint but his purposefulness.

Where were the Naturalists?

Harry searched for several years.

The press?

But there were no Naturalists visible on the telescreens. The news and the newsmakers reflected a national philosophy adopted many generations ago by the Founding Fathers of mass-communication in their infinite wisdom—"*What's good for General Motors is good for the country.*" And according to them, everything happening was good for the country; that was the cardinal precept in the science of autobuyology. There were no Arnold Ritchies left any more, and the printed newzine seemed to have vanished.

The clergy?

Individual churches with congregations in physical attendance, seemed difficult to find. Telepreachers still appeared regularly every Sunday, but their scripts—like everyone else's—had been processed in advance. Denominationalism and sectarianism had waned, too; all of these performers seemed very much alike, in that they were vigorous, forthright, inspiring champions of the *status quo.*

The scientists?

But the scientists were a part of the government, and the government was a one-party system, and the system supported the nation and the nation supported the scientists. Of course, there were still private laboratories subsidized for industrial purposes, but the men who worked in them seemed singularly disinterested in social problems. In a way, Harry could understand their position. It isn't likely that a dedicated scientist, a man whose specialized research has won him a Nobel Prize for creating a new detergent, will be worldly enough to face unpleasant realities beyond the walls of his antiseptic sanctum. After all, there was precedent for such isolationism—did the sainted Betty Crocker ever enlist in any crusades? As for physicians, psychiatrists and mass-psychologists, they were the very ones who formed the hard core of Leffingwell's support.

The educators, then?

Vocational Apt was a part of the government. And the poor pedagogues, who had spent generations hacking their way out of the blackboard jungles, were only too happy to welcome the notion of a coming millennium when their small charges would be still smaller. Even though formal schooling, for most youngsters, terminated at fourteen, there was still the problem of overcrowding. Telescreening and teletesting techniques were a help, but the problem was essentially a physical one. And Leffingwell was providing a physical solution. Besides, the educators had been themselves educated, through Vocational Apt. And while they, and the government, fervently upheld the principle of freedom of speech, they had to draw the line somewhere. As everyone knows, freedom of speech does not mean freedom to *criticize*.

Business men?

Perhaps there were some disgruntled souls in the commercial community, whose secret heroes were the oil tycoons of a bygone era or the old-time Stock Exchange clan united under the totems of the bull or the bear. But the day of the rugged individualist was long departed; only the flabby individualist remained. And he had the forms to fill out and the inspectors to contend with, and the rationing to worry about and the taxes to meet and the quotas to fulfill. But in the long run, he managed. The business man worked for the government, but the government also worked for him. His position was protected. And if the government said the Leff Shots would solve the overpopulation problem—*without* cutting down the number of consumers—well, was that really so bad? Why, in a generation or so there'd be even *more* customers! That meant increased property values, too.

It took Harry several years to realize he'd never find Naturalists organized for group action. The capacity for group action had vanished as the size of the group increased. All interests were interdependent; the old civic, fraternal, social and anti-social societies had no present purpose any more. And the once-familiar rallying-points—whether they represented idealistic humanitarianism or crass self-interest—had vanished in the crowd. Patriotism, racialism, unionism, had all been lost in a moiling megalopolitanism.

There were protests, of course. The mothers objected, some of them. Ag Culture, in particular, ran into difficulties with women who revived the quaint custom of "going on strike" against the Leff Law and refused to take their shots. But it was all on the individual level, and quickly coped with. Government medical authorities met the women at checkup time and demonstrated that the Leff Law had teeth in it. Teeth, and scalpels. The rebellious women were not subdued, slain, or segregated—they were merely sterilized. Perhaps more would have come of this if their men had backed them up; but the men, by and large, were realists. Having a kid was a headache these days. This new business of injections wasn't so bad, when you came right down to it. There'd still be youngsters around, and you'd get the same allotment for extra living space—only the way it worked out, there'd be more room and the kids would eat less. Pretty good deal. And it wasn't as if the young ones were harmed. Some of them seemed to be a lot smarter than ordinary—like on some of the big quizshows, youngsters of eight and nine were winning all those big prizes. Bright little ones. Of course, these must be the ones raised in the first special school the government had set up.

They said old Leffingwell, the guy who invented the shots, was running it himself. Sort of experimenting to see how this new crop of kids would make out....

It was when Harry learned about the school that he knew what he must do.

And if nobody else would help him, he'd act on his own. There might not be any help from organized society, but he still had disorganized society to turn to.

He spent the next two years and the last of his money finding a way. The pattern of criminality had changed, too, and it was no easy matter to find the assistance he needed. About the only group crime still flourishing was hijacking; it took him a long while to locate a small under-cover outfit which operated around St. Louie and arrange to obtain a helicopter and pilot. Getting hold of the rifle was still more difficult, but he managed. And by the time everything was assembled, he'd found out what he needed to know about Dr. Leffingwell and his school.

As he'd suspected, the school was located in the old canyon, right in the same buildings which had once served as experimental units. How many youngsters were there, Harry didn't know. Maybe Manschoff was still on the staff, and maybe they'd brought in a whole new staff. These things didn't matter. What mattered was that Leffingwell was on the premises. And a man who knew his way about, a man who worked alone and to a single purpose, could reach him.

Thus it was that Harry Collins crouched behind the boulder that bright May morning and waited for Dr. Leffingwell to appear. The helicopter had dropped him at the upper end of the canyon the day before, giving him a chance to reconnoitre and familiarize himself with the terrain once again. He'd located Leffingwell's quarters, even seen the man through one of the lower windows. Harry had no trouble recognizing him; the face was only too familiar from a thousand 'casts viewed on a thousand screens. Inevitably, some time today, he'd emerge from the building. And when he did, Harry would be waiting.

He shifted behind the rocks and stretched his legs. Twelve years had passed, and now he'd come full circle. The whole business had started here, and here it must end. That was simple justice.

And it is justice, Harry told himself. *It's not revenge.* Because there'd be no point to revenge; that was only melodramatic nonsense. He was no Monte Cristo, come to wreak vengeance on his cruel oppressors. And he was no madman, no victim of a monomaniacal obsession. What he was doing was the result of lengthy and logical consideration.

If Harry Collins, longtime fugitive from a government treatment center, tried to take his story to the people, he'd be silenced without a hearing. But his story must be heard. There was only one way to arrest the attention of a nation—with the report of a rifle.

A bullet in Leffingwell's brain; that was the solution of the problem. Overnight the assassin would become a national figure. They'd undoubtedly try him and undoubtedly condemn him, but first he'd have his day in court. He'd get a chance to speak out. He'd give all the voiceless, unorganized victims of the Leff Law a reason for rebellion—and offer them an example. If Leffingwell had to die, it would be in a good cause. Moreover, he deserved to die. Hadn't he killed men, women, infants, without mercy?

But it's not revenge, Harry repeated. *And I know what I'm doing. Maybe I was disturbed before, but I'm sane now. Perfectly logical. Perfectly calm. Perfectly controlled.*

Yes, and now his sane, logical, calm, controlled eyes noted that the distant door was opening, and he sighted through the 'scope and brought his sane, logical, calm, controlled hand up along the barrel to the trigger. He could see the two men emerging, and the shorter, plumper of the two was Leffingwell. He squinted at the high forehead with its receding hairline; it was a perfect target. A little squeeze now and he knew what would happen. In his sane, logical, calm, controlled mind he could visualize the way the black hole would appear in the center of that forehead, while behind it would be the torn and dripping redness flecked with gray—

"What are you doing?"

Harry whirled, staring; staring down at the infant who stood smiling beside him. It *was* an infant, that was obvious enough, and implicit in the diminutive stature, the delicate limbs and the oversized head. But infants do not wear the clothing of pre-adolescent boys, they do not enunciate with clarity, they do not stare coolly and knowingly at their elders. They do not say, "Why do you want to harm Dr. Leffingwell?"

Harry gazed into the wide eyes. He couldn't speak.

"You're sick, aren't you?" the child persisted. "Let me call the doctor. He can help you."

Harry swung the rifle around. "I'll give you just ten seconds to clear out of here before I shoot."

The child shook his head. Then he took a step forward. "You wouldn't hurt me," he said, gravely. "You're just sick. That's why you talk this way."

Harry leveled the rifle. "I'm not sick," he muttered. "I know what I'm doing. And I know all about you, too. You're one of them, aren't you? One of the first of Leffingwell's brood of illegitimates."

The child took another step forward. "I'm not illegitimate," he said. "I know who I am. I've seen the records. My name is Harry Collins."

Somewhere the rifle exploded, the bullet hurtling harmlessly overhead. But Harry didn't hear it. All he could hear, exploding in his own brain as he went down into darkness, was the sane, logical, calm, controlled voice of his son.

7. Michael Cavendish—2027

Mike was just coming through the clump of trees when the boy began to wave at him. He shifted the clumsy old Jeffrey .475, cursing the weight as he quickened his pace. But there was no help for it, he had to carry the gun himself. None of the boys were big enough.

He wondered what it had been like in the old days, when you could get fullsized bearers. There used to be game all over the place, too, and a white hunter was king.

And what was there left now? Nothing but pygmies, all of them, scurrying around and beating the brush for dibatags and gerenuks. When he was still a boy, Mike had seen the last of the big antelopes go; the last of the wildebeestes and zebra, too. Then the carnivores followed—the lions and the leopards. *Simba* was dead, and just as well. These natives would never dare to come out of the villages if they knew any lions were left. Most of them had gone to Cape and the other cities anyway; handling cattle was too much of a chore, except on a government farm. Those cows looked like moving mountains alongside the average boy.

Of course there were still some of the older generation left; Kikiyu and even a few Watusi. But the free inoculations had begun many years ago, and the life-cycle moved at an accelerated pace here. Natives grew old and died at thirty; they matured at fifteen. Now, with the shortage of game, the elders perished still more swiftly and only the young remained outside the cities and the farm projects.

Mike smiled as he waited for the boy to come up to him. He wasn't smiling at the boy—he was smiling at himself, for being here. He ought to be in Cape, too, or Kenyarobi. Damned silly, this business of being a white hunter, when there was nothing left to hunt.

But somehow he'd stayed on, since Dad died. There were a few compensations. At least here in the forests a man could still move about a bit, taste privacy and solitude and the strange, exotic tropical fruit called loneliness. Even *that* was vanishing today.

It was compensation enough, perhaps, for lugging this damned Jeffrey. Mike tried to remember the last time he'd fired it at a living target. A year, two years? Yes, almost two. That gorilla up in Ruwenzori country. At least the boys swore it was *ingagi.* He hadn't hit it, anyway. Got away in the darkness. Probably he'd been shooting at a shadow. There were no more gorillas—maybe *they* had been taking the shots, too. Perhaps they'd all turned into rhesus monkeys.

Mike watched the boy run towards him. It was a good five hundred yards from the river bank, and the short brown legs couldn't move very swiftly. He wondered what it felt like to be small. One's sense of proportion must be different. And that, in turn, would affect one's sense of values. What values applied to the world about you when you were only three feet high?

Mike wouldn't know. He was a big man—almost five feet seven.

Sometimes Mike reflected on what things might be like if he'd been born, say, twenty years later. By that time almost everyone would be a product of Leff shots, and he'd be no exception. He might stay with people his own age in Kenyarobi without feeling self-conscious, clumsy, conspicuous. Pressed, he had to admit that was part of the reason he preferred to remain out here at Dad's old place now. He could tolerate the stares of the natives, but whenever he ventured into a city he felt awkward under the scrutiny of the young people. The way those teen-agers looked up at him made him feel a monster, rather.

Better to endure the monotony, the emptiness out here. Yes, and wait for a chance to hunt. Even though, nine times out of ten, it turned out to be a wild goose-chase. During the past year or so Mike had hunted nothing but legends and rumors, spent his time stalking shadows.

Then the villagers had come to him, three days ago, with their wild story. Even when he heard it, he realized it must be pure fable. And the more they insisted, the more they protested, the more he realized it simply couldn't be.

Still, he'd come. Anything to experience some action, anything to create the illusion of purpose, of—

"*Tembo!*" shrieked the boy, excited beyond all pretense of caution. "Up ahead, in river. You come quick, you see!"

No. It couldn't be. The government surveys were thorough. The last record of a specimen dated back over a half-dozen years ago. It was impossible that any survivors remained. And all during the safari these past days, not a sign or a print or a spoor.

"*Tembo!*" shrilled the boy. "Come quick!"

Mike cradled the gun and started forward. The other bearers shuffled behind him, unable to keep pace because of their short legs and—he suspected—unwilling to do so for fear of what might lie ahead.

Halfway towards the river bank, Mike halted. Now he could hear the rumbling, the unmistakable rumbling. And now he could smell the rank mustiness borne on the hot breeze. Well, at least he was down-wind.

The boy behind him trembled, eyes wide. He *had* seen something, all right. Maybe just a crocodile, though. Still some crocs around. And he doubted if a young native would know the difference.

Nevertheless, Mike felt a sudden surge of unfamiliar excitement, half expectancy and half fear. *Something* wallowed in the river; something that rumbled and exuded the stench of life.

Now they were approaching the trees bordering the bank. Mike checked his gun carefully. Then he advanced until his body was aligned with the trees. From here he could see and not be seen. He could peer down at the river—or the place where the river had been, during the rainy season long past. Now it was nothing but a mudwallow under the glaring sun; a huge mudwallow, pitted with deep, circular indentations and dotted with dung.

But in the middle of it stood *tembo.*

Tembo was a mountain, *tembo* was a black block of breathing basalt. *Tembo* roared and snorted and rolled red eyes.

Mike gasped.

He was a white hunter, but he'd never seen a bull elephant before. And this one stood eleven feet at the shoulders if it stood an inch; the biggest creature walking the face of the earth.

It had risen from the mud, abandoned its wallowing as its trunk curled about, sensitive to the unfamiliar scent of man. Its ears rose like the outspread wings of some gigantic jungle bat. Mike could see the flies buzzing around the ragged edges. He stared at the great tusks that were veined and yellowed and broken—once men had hunted elephants for ivory, he remembered.

But how could they? Even with guns, how had they dared to confront a moving mountain? Mike tried to swallow, but his throat was dry. The stock slipped through his clammy hands.

"Shoot!" implored the boy beside him. "You shoot, now!"

Mike gazed down. The elephant was aware of him. It turned deliberately, staring up the bank as it swayed on the four black pillars of its legs. Mike could see its eyes, set in a mass of grayish wrinkles. The eyes had recognized him.

They knew, he realized. The eyes knew all about him; who he was and what he was and what he had come here to do. The eyes had seen man before—perhaps long before Mike was born. They understood everything; the gun and the presence and the purpose.

"Shoot!" the boy cried, not bothering to hold his voice down any longer. For the elephant was moving slowly towards the side of the wallow, moving deliberately to firmer footing, and the boy was afraid. Mike was afraid, too, but he couldn't shoot.

"No," he murmured. "Let him go. I can't kill him."

"You must," the boy said. "You promise. Look—all the meat. Meat for two, three villages."

Mike shook his head. "I can't do it," he said. "That isn't meat. That's life. Bigger life than we are. Don't you understand? Oh, the bloody hell with it! Come on."

The boy wasn't listening to him. He was watching the elephant. And now he started to tremble.

For the elephant was moving up onto solid ground. It moved slowly, daintily, almost mincing as its legs sampled the surface of the shore. Then it looked up and this time there was no doubt as to the direction of its gaze—it stared intently at Mike and the boy on the bank. Its ears fanned, then flared. Suddenly the elephant raised its trunk and trumpeted fiercely.

And then, lowering the black battering-ram of its head, the beast came forward. A deceptively slow lope, a scarcely accelerated trot, and then all at once it was moving swiftly, swiftly and surely and inexorably towards them. The angle of the bank was not steep and the elephant's speed never slackened on the slope. Its right shoulder struck a sapling and the sapling splintered. It was crashing forward in full charge. Again it trumpeted, trunk extended like a flail of doom.

"Shoot!" screamed the boy.

Mike didn't want to shoot. He wanted to run. He wanted to flee the mountain, flee the incredible breathing bulk of this grotesque giant. But he was a white hunter, he was a man, and a man is not a beast; a man does not run away from life in any shape or size.

The trunk came up. Mike raised the gun. He heard the monster roar, far away, and then he heard another sound that must be the gun's discharge, and something hit him in the shoulder and knocked him down. Recoil? Yes, because the elephant wasn't there any more; he could hear the crashing and thrashing down below, over the rim of the river bank.

Mike stood up. He saw the boy running now, running back to the bearers huddled along the edge of the trail.

He rubbed his shoulder, picked up his gun, reloaded. The sounds from below had ceased. Slowly, Mike advanced to the lip of the bank and stared down.

The bull elephant had fallen and rolled into the wallow once more. It had taken a direct hit, just beneath the right ear, and even as Mike watched, its trunk writhed feebly like a dying serpent, then fell forward into the mud. The gigantic ears twitched, then flickered and flopped, and the huge body rolled and settled.

Suddenly Mike began to cry.

Damn it, he hadn't *wanted* to shoot. If the elephant hadn't charged like that—

But the elephant *had* to charge. Just as he *had* to shoot. That was the whole secret. The secret of life. And the secret of death, too.

Mike turned away, facing the east. Kenyarobi was east, and he'd be going there now. Nothing to hold him here in the forests any longer. He wouldn't even wait for the big feast. To hell with elephant-meat, anyway. His hunting days were over.

Mike walked slowly up the trail to the waiting boys.

And behind him, in the wallow, the flies settled down on the lifeless carcass of the last elephant in the world.

---

8. Harry Collins—2029

The guards at Stark Falls were under strict orders not to talk. Each prisoner here was exercised alone in a courtyard runway, and meals were served in the cells. The cells were comfortable enough, and while there were no telescreens, books were available—genuine, old-style books which must have been preserved from libraries dismantled fifty years ago or more. Harry Collins found no titles dated later than 1975. Every day or so an attendant wheeled around a cart piled high with the dusty volumes. Harry read to pass the time.

At first he kept anticipating his trial, but after a while he almost forgot about that possibility. And it was well over a year before he got a chance to tell his story to anyone.

When his opportunity came, his audience did not consist of judge or jury, doctor, lawyer or penologist. He spoke only to Richard Wade, a fellow-prisoner who had been thrust into the adjoining cell on the evening of October 11th, 2013.

Harry spoke haltingly at first, but as he progressed the words came more easily, and emotion lent its own eloquence. His unseen auditor on the other side of the wall did not interrupt or question him; it was enough, for Harry, that there *was* someone to listen at last.

"So it wasn't a bit like I'd expected," he concluded. "No trial, no publicity. I've never seen Leffingwell again, nor Manschoff. Nobody questioned me. By the time I recovered consciousness, I was here in prison. Buried alive."

Richard Wade spoke slowly, for the first time. "You're lucky. They might have shot you down on the spot."

"That's just what bothers me," Harry told him. "Why didn't they kill me? Why lock me up *incommunicado* this way? There aren't many prisons left these days, with food and space at such a premium."

"There are *no* prisons left at all—officially," Wade said. "Just as there are no longer any cemeteries. But important people are still given private burials and their remains secretly preserved. All a matter of influence."

"I've no influence. I'm not important. Wouldn't you think they'd consider it risky to keep me alive, under the circumstances? If there'd ever be an investigation—"

"Who would investigate? Not the government, surely."

"But suppose there's a political turnover. Suppose Congress want to make capital of the situation?"

"There is no Congress."

Harry gasped. "No Congress?"

"As of last month. It was dissolved. Henceforth we are governed by the Cabinet, with authority delegated to department heads."

"But that's preposterous! Nobody'd stand still for something like that!"

"They did stand still, most of them. After a year of careful preparation—of wholesale *exposes* of Congressional graft and corruption and inefficiency. Turned out that Congress was the villain all along; the Senators and Representatives had finagled tariff-barriers and restrictive trade-agreements which kept our food supply down. They were opposing international federation. In plain language, people were sold a bill of goods—get rid of Congress and you'll have more food. That did it."

"But you'd think the politicians themselves would realize they were cutting their own throats! The state legislatures and the governors—"

"Legislatures were dissolved by the same agreement," Wade went on. "There are no states any more; just governmental districts. Based upon sensible considerations of area and population. This isn't the old-time expanding economy based on obsolescence and conspicuous consumption. The primary problem at the moment is sheer survival. In a way, the move makes sense. Old-fashioned political machinery couldn't cope with the situation; there's no time for debate when instantaneous decisions are necessary to national welfare. You've heard how civil liberties were suspended during the old wars. Well, there's a war on right now; a war against hunger, a war against the forces of fecundity. In another dozen years or so, when the Leff shot generation is fullgrown and a lot of the elderly have died off, the tensions will ease. Meanwhile, quick action is necessary. Arbitrary action."

"But you're defending dictatorship!"

Richard Wade made a sound which is usually accompanied by a derisive shrug. "Am I? Well, I didn't when I was outside. And that's why I'm here now."

Harry Collins cleared his throat. "What did you do?"

"If you refer to my profession, I was a scripter. If you refer to my alleged criminal activity, I made the error of thinking the way you do, and the worse error of attempting to inject such attitudes in my scripts. Seems that when Congress was formally dissolved, there was some notion of preparing a timely show—a sort of historical review of the body, using old film clips. What my superiors had in mind was a comedy of errors; a cavalcade of mistakes and misdeeds showing just why we were better off without supporting a political sideshow. Well, I carried out the assignment and edited the films, but when I drafted a rough commentary, I made the mistake of taking both a pro and con slant. Nothing like that ever reached the telescreens, of course, but what I did was promptly noted. They came for me at once and hustled me off here. I didn't get a hearing or a trial, either."

"But why didn't they execute you? Or—" Harry hesitated—"is that what you expect?"

"Why didn't they execute *you*?" Wade shot back. He was silent for a moment before continuing. "No, I don't expect anything like that, now. They'd have done it on the spot if they intended to do so at all. No, I've got another idea about people like you and myself. And about some of the Congressmen and Senators who dropped out of sight, too. I think we're being stockpiled."

"Stockpiled?"

"It's all part of a plan. Give me a little time to think. We can talk again, later." Wade chuckled once more. "Looks as if there'll be ample opportunity in the future."

And there was. In the months ahead, Harry spoke frequently with his friend behind the wall. He never saw him—prisoners at Stark Falls were exercised separately, and there was no group assembly or recreation. Surprisingly adequate meals were served in surprisingly comfortable cells. In the matter of necessities, Harry had no complaints. And now that he had someone to talk to, the time seemed to go more swiftly.

He learned a great deal about Richard Wade during the next few years. Mostly, Wade liked to reminisce about the old days. He talked about working for the networks—the *commercial* networks, privately owned, which flourished before the government took over communications media in the '80s.

"That's where you got your start, eh?" Harry asked.

"Lord, no, boy! I'm a lot more ancient than you think. Why, I'm pushing sixty-five. Born in 1940. That's right, during World War II. I can almost remember the atomic bomb, and I sure as hell remember the sputniks. It was a crazy period, let me tell you. The pessimists worried about the Russians blowing us up, and the optimists were sure we had a glorious future in the conquest of space. Ever hear that old fable about the blind men examining an elephant? Well, that's the way most people were; each of them groping around and trying to determine the exact shape of things to come. A few of us even made a little money from it for a while, writing science fiction. That's how I got my start."

"You were a writer?"

"Sold my first story when I was eighteen or so. Kept on writing off and on for almost twenty years. Of course, Robertson's thermo-nuc formula came along in '75, and after that everything went to pot. It knocked out the chances of future war, but it also knocked out the interest in speculation or escape-fiction. So I moved over into television for a while, and stayed with it. But the old science fiction was fun while it lasted. Ever read any of it?"

"No," Harry admitted. "That was all before my time. Tell me, though—did any of it make sense? I mean, did some of those writers foresee what was really going to happen?"

"There were plenty of penny prophets and nickel Nostradamuses," Wade told him. "But as I said, most of them were assuming war with the Communists or a new era of space travel. Since Communism collapsed and space flight was just an expensive journey to a dead end and dead worlds, it follows that the majority of fictional futures were founded on fallacies. And all the rest of the extrapolations dealt with superficial social manifestations.

"For example, they wrote about civilizations dominated by advertising and mass-motivation techniques. It's true that during my childhood this seemed to be a logical trend—but once demand exceeded supply, the whole mechanism of *stimulating* demand, which was advertising's chief function, bogged down. And mass-motivation techniques, today, are dedicated almost entirely to maintaining minimum resistance to a system insuring our survival.

"Another popular idea was based on the notion of an expanding matriarchy—a gerontomatriarchy, rather, in which older women would take control. In an age when women outlived men by a number of years, this seemed possible. Now, of course, shortened working hours and medical advances have equalized the life-span. And since private property has become less and less of a factor in dominating our collective destinies, it hardly matters whether the male or the female has the upper hand.

"Then there was the common theory that technological advances would result in a push-button society, where automatons would do all the work. And so they might—if we had an unlimited supply of raw materials to produce robots, and unlimited power-sources to activate them. As we now realize, atomic power cannot be utilized on a minute scale.

"Last, but not least, there was the concept of a medically-orientated system, with particular emphasis on psychotherapy, neurosurgery, and parapsychology. The world was going to be run by telepaths, psychosis eliminated by brainwashing, intellect developed by hypnotic suggestion. It sounded great—but the conquest of physical disease has occupied the medical profession almost exclusively.

"No, what they all seemed to overlook, with only a few exceptions, was the population problem. You can't run a world through advertising when there are so many people that there aren't enough goods to go around anyway. You can't turn it over to big business when big government has virtually absorbed all of the commercial and industrial functions, just to cope with an ever-growing demand. A matriarchy loses its meaning when the individual family unit changes character, under the stress of an increasing population-pressure which eliminates the old-fashioned home, family circle, and social pattern. And the more we must conserve dwindling natural resources for people, the less we can expend on experimentation with robots and machinery. As for the psychologist-dominated society, there are just too many patients and not enough physicians. I don't have to remind you that the military caste lost its chance of control when war disappeared, and that religion is losing ground every day. Class-lines are vanishing, and racial distinctions will be going next. The old idea of a World Federation is becoming more and more practical. Once the political barriers are down, miscegenation will finish the job. But nobody seemed to foresee this particular future. They all made the mistake of worrying about the hydrogen-bomb instead of the sperm-bomb."

Harry nodded thoughtfully, although Wade couldn't see his response. "But isn't it true that there's a little bit of each of these concepts in our actual situation today?" he asked. "I mean, government and business *are* virtually one and the same, and they do use propaganda techniques to control all media. As for scientific research, look at how we've rebuilt our cities and developed synthetics for food and fuel and clothing and shelter. When it comes to medicine, there's Leffingwell and his inoculations. Isn't that all along the lines of your early science fiction?"

"Where's your Underground?" Richard Wade demanded.

"My *what*?"

"Your Underground," Wade repeated. "Hell, every science fiction yarn about a future society had its Underground! That was the whole gimmick in the plot. The hero was a conformist who tangled with the social order—come to think of it, that's what *you* did, years ago. Only instead of becoming an impotent victim of the system, he'd meet up with the Underground Movement. Not some sourball like your friend Ritchie, who tried to operate on his own hook, without real plans or system, but a complete *sub rosa* organization, bent on starting a revolution and taking over. There'd be wise old priests and wise old crooks and wise old officers and wise old officials, all playing a double game and planning a *coup*. Spies all over the place, get me? And in no time at all, our hero would be playing tag with the top figures in the government. That's how it worked out in all the stories.

"But what happens in real life? What happened to you, for example? You fell for a series of stupid tricks, stupidly perpetrated—because the people in power *are* people, and not the kind of synthetic super-intellects dreamed up by frustrated fiction-fabricators. You found out that the logical candidates to constitute an Underground were the Naturalists; again, they were just ordinary individuals with no genius for organization. As for coming in contact with key figures, you were actually on hand when Leffingwell completed his experiments. And you came back, years later, to hunt him down. Very much in the heroic tradition, I admit. But you never saw the man except through the telescopic sights of your rifle. That was the end of it. No modern-day Machiavelli has hauled you in to play cat-and-mouse games with you, and no futuristic Freud has bothered to wash your brain or soft-soap your subconscious. You just aren't that important, Collins."

"But they put me in a special prison. Why?"

"Who knows? They put me here, too."

"You said something once, about stockpiling us. What did you mean?"

"Well, it was just an old science fiction idea, I suppose. I'll tell you about it tomorrow, eh?"

And so the matter—and Harry Collins—rested for the night.

The next day Richard Wade was gone.

Harry called to him and there was no answer. And he cried out and he cursed and he paced his cell and he walked alone in the courtyard and he begged the impassive guards for information, and he sweated and he talked to himself and he counted the days and he lost count of the days.

Then, all at once, there was another prisoner in the adjacent cell, and his name was William Chang, and he was a biologist. He was reticent about the crime he had committed, but quite voluble about the crimes committed by others in the world outside. Much of what he said, about genes and chromosomes and recessive characteristics and mutation, seemed incomprehensible to Harry. But in their talks, one thing emerged clearly enough—Chang was concerned for the future of the race. "Leffingwell should have waited," he said. "It's the *second* generation that will be important. As I tried to tell my people—"

"Is that why you're here?"

Chang sighed. "I suppose so. They wouldn't listen, of course. Overpopulation has always been the curse of Asia, and this seemed to be such an obvious solution. But who knows? The time may come when they need men like myself."

"So you were stockpiled too."

"What's that?"

Harry told him about Richard Wade's remarks, and together they tried to puzzle out the theory behind them.

But not for long. Because once again Harry Collins awoke in the morning to find the adjoining cell empty, and once again he was alone for a long time.

At last a new neighbor came. His name was Lars Neilstrom. Neilstrom talked to him of ships and shoes and sealing-wax and the thousand and one things men will discuss in their loneliness and frustration, including—inevitably—their reasons for being here.

Neilstrom had been an instructor under Vocational Apt, and he was at a loss to explain his presence at Stark Falls. When Harry spoke of the stockpiling theory, his fellow-prisoner demurred. "It's more like Kafka than science fiction," he said. "But then, I don't suppose you've ever read any Kafka."

"Yes, I have," Harry told him. "Since I came here I've done nothing but read old books. Lately they've been giving me microscans. I've been studying up on biology and genetics; talking to Chang got me interested. In fact, I'm really going in for self-education. There's nothing else to do."

"Self-education! That's the only method left nowadays." Neilstrom sounded bitter. "I don't know what's going to become of our heritage of knowledge in the future. I'm not speaking of technological skill; so-called scientific information is carefully preserved. But the humanities are virtually lost. The concept of the well-rounded individual is forgotten. And when I think of the crisis to come—"

"What crisis?"

"A new generation is growing up. Ten or fifteen years from now we'll have succeeded in erasing political and racial and religious divisions. But there'll be a new and more dangerous differentiation; a *physical* one. What do you think will happen when half the world is around six feet tall and the other half under three?"

"I can't imagine."

"Well, I can. The trouble is, most people don't realize what the problem will be. Things have moved too swiftly. Why, there were more changes in the last hundred years than in the previous thousand! And the rate of acceleration increases. Up until now, we've been concerned about too rapid technological development. But what we have to worry about is social development."

"Most people have been conditioned to conform."

"Yes. That's our job in Vocational Apt. But the system only works when there's a single standard of conformity. In a few years there'll be a double one, based on size. What then?"

Harry wanted some time to consider the matter, but the question was never answered. Because Lars Neilstrom went away in the night, as had his predecessors before him. And in succeeding interludes, Harry came to know a half-dozen other transient occupants of the cell next to his. They came from all over, and they had many things to discuss, but always there was the problem of *why* they were there—and the memory of Richard Wade's premise concerning stockpiling.

There came a time when the memory of Richard Wade merged with the memory of Arnold Ritchie. The past was a dim montage of life at the agency and the treatment center and the ranch, a recollection of lying on the river bank with women in attitudes of opisthotonos or of lying against the boulders with a rifle.

Somewhere there was an image of a child's wide eyes and a voice saying, "My name is Harry Collins." But that seemed very far away. What was real was the cell and the years of talking and reading the microscans and trying to find a pattern.

Harry found himself describing it all to a newcomer who said his name was Austin—a soft-voiced man who became a resident of the next cell one day in 2029. And eventually he came to Wade's theory.

"Maybe there were a few wiser heads who foresaw a coming crisis," he concluded. "Maybe they anticipated a time when they might need a few nonconformists. People like ourselves who haven't been passive or persuaded. Maybe we're the government's insurance policy. If an emergency arises, we'll be freed."

"And then what would *you* do?" Austin asked, softly. "You're against the system, aren't you?"

"Yes. But I'm *for* survival." Harry Collins spoke slowly, thoughtfully. "You see, I've learned something through the years of study and contact here. Rebellion is not the answer."

"You hated Leffingwell."

"Yes, I did, until I realized that all this was inevitable. Leffingwell is not a villain and neither is any given individual, in or out of government. Our road to hell has been paved with only the very best of intentions. Killing the engineers and contractors will not get us off that road, and we're all on it together. We'll have to find a way of changing the direction of our journey. The young people will be too anxious to merely rush blindly ahead. Most of my generation will be sheeplike, moving as part of the herd, because of their conditioning. Only we old-time rebels will be capable of plotting a course. A course for all of us."

"What about your son?" Austin asked.

"I'm thinking of him," Harry Collins answered. "Of him, and of all the others. Maybe he does not need me. Maybe none of them need me. Maybe it's all an illusion. But if the time ever comes, I'll be ready. And meanwhile, I can hope."

"The time has come," Austin said, gently.

And then he was standing, miraculously enough, outside his cell and before the door to Harry's cell, and the door was opening. And once again Harry stared into the wide eyes he remembered so well—the same wide eyes, set in the face of a fullgrown man. A fullgrown man, three feet tall. He stood up, shakily, as the man held out his hand and said, "Hello, Father."

"But I don't understand—"

"I've waited a long time for this moment. I had to talk to you, find out how you really felt, so that I'd be sure. Now you're ready to join us."

"What's happening? What do you want with me?"

"We'll talk later." Harry's son smiled. "Right now, I'm taking you home."

9. Eric Donovan—2031

Eric was glad to get to the office and shut the door. Lately he'd had this feeling whenever he went out, this feeling that people were staring at him. It wasn't just his imagination: they did stare. Every younger person over a yard high got stared at nowadays, as if they were freaks. And it wasn't just the staring that got him down, either.

Sometimes they muttered and mumbled, and sometimes they called names. Eric didn't mind stuff like "dirty Naturalist." That he could understand—once upon a time, way back, everybody who was against the Leff Law was called a Naturalist. And before that it had still another meaning, or so he'd been told. Today, of course, it just meant anyone who was over five feet tall.

No, he could take the ordinary name-calling, all right. But sometimes they said other things. They used words nobody ever uses unless they really hate you, want to kill you. And that was at the bottom of it, Eric knew. They did hate him, they *did* want to kill him.

Was he a coward? Perhaps. But it wasn't just Eric's imagination. You never saw anything about such things on the telescreens, but Naturalists were being killed every day. The older people were still in the majority, but the youngsters were coming up fast. And there were so many *more* of them. Besides, they were more active, and this created the illusion that there were Yardsticks everywhere.

Eric sat down behind his desk, grinning. *Yardsticks*. When he was a kid it had been just the other way around. He and the rest of them who didn't get shots in those early days considered themselves to be the normal ones. And *they* did the name-calling. Names like "runt" and "half-pint" and "midgie." But the most common name was the one that stuck—Yardstick. That used to be the worst insult of all.

But now it wasn't an insult any more. Being taller was the insult. Being a dirty Naturalist or a son-of-a-Naturalist. Times certainly had changed.

Eric glanced at the communicator. Almost noon, and it had not flicked yet. Here he'd been beaming these big offers, you'd think he'd get some response to an expensive beaming program, but no. Maybe that was the trouble—nobody liked *big* things any more. Everything was small.

He shifted uneasily in his chair. That was one consolation, at least; he still had old-time furniture. Getting to be harder and harder to find stuff that fitted him these days. Seemed like most of the firms making furniture and bedding and household appliances were turning out the small stuff for the younger generation. Cheaper to make, less material, and more demand for it. Government allocated size priorities to the manufacturers.

It was even murder to ride public transportation because of the space-reductions. Eric drove his own jetter. Besides, that way was safer. Crowded into a liner with a gang of Yardsticks, with only a few other Naturalists around, there might be trouble.

Oh, it was getting to be a Yardstick world, and no mistake. Smaller furniture, smaller meals, smaller sizes in clothing, smaller buildings—

That reminded Eric of something and he frowned again. Dammit, why didn't the communicator flick? He should be getting some kind of inquiries. Hell, he was practically *giving* the space away!

But there was only silence, as there had been all during this past week. That's why he let Lorette go. Sweet girl, but there was no work for her here any more. No work, and no pay, either. Besides, the place spooked her. She'd been the one who suggested leaving, really.

"Eric, I'm sorry, but I just can't take this any more. All alone in this huge building—it's curling my toes!"

At first he tried to talk her out of it. "Don't be silly, luscious! There's Bernstein, down on ten, and Saltonstall above us, and Wallaby and Son on fourteen, I tell you, this place is coming back to life, I can feel it! I'll beam for tenants next week, you'll see—"

Actually he'd been talking against his own fear and Lorette must have known it. Anyway, she left. And now he was here alone.

Alone.

Eric didn't like the sound of that word. Or the absence of sound behind it. Three other tenants in a ninety-story building. Three other tenants in a place that had once held three thousand. Why, fifty years ago, when this place went up, you couldn't buy a vacancy. Where had the crowds gone to?

He knew the answer, of course. The Leff shots had created the new generation of Yardsticks, and they lived in their own world. Their shrunken, dehydrated world of doll-houses and miniatures. They'd deserted the old-fashioned skyscrapers and cut the big apartment buildings up into tiny cubicles; two could occupy the space formerly reserved for one.

That had been the purpose of the Leff shots in the first place—to put an end to overcrowding and conserve on resources. Well, it had worked out. Worked out too perfectly for people like Eric Donovan. Eric Donovan, rental agent for a building nobody wanted any more; a ninety-storey mausoleum. And nobody could collect rent from ghosts.

Ghosts.

Eric damned near jumped through the ceiling when the door opened and this man walked in. He was tall and towheaded. Eric stared; there was something vaguely familiar about his face. Something about those ears, that was it, those ears. No, it couldn't be, it wasn't possible—

Eric stood up and held out his hand. "I'm Donovan," he said.

The towheaded man smiled and nodded. "Yes, I know. Don't you remember me?"

"I thought I knew you from someplace. You wouldn't be—Sam Wolzek?"

The towheaded man's smile became a broad grin. "That's not what you were going to say, Eric. You were going to say 'Handle-head,' weren't you? Well, go on, say it. I don't mind. I've been called a lot worse things since we were kids together."

"I can't believe it," Eric murmured. "It's really you! Old Handle-head Wolzek! And after all these years, turning up to rent an office from me. Well, what do you know!"

"I didn't come here to rent an office."

"Oh? Then—"

"It was your name that brought me. I recognized it on the beamings."

"Then this is a social call, eh? Well, that's good. I don't get much company these days. Sit down, have a reef."

Wolzek sat down but refused the smoke. "I know quite a bit about your setup," he said. "You and your three tenants. It's tough, Eric."

"Oh, things could be worse." Eric forced a laugh. "It isn't as if my bucks depended on the number of tenants in the building. Government subsidizes this place. I'm sure of a job as long as I live."

"As long as you live." Wolzek stared at him in a way he didn't like. "And just how long do you figure that to be?"

"I'm only twenty-six," Eric answered. "According to statistics, that gives me maybe another sixty years."

"Statistics!" Wolzek said it like a dirty word. "Your life-expectancy isn't determined by statistics any more. I say you don't have sixty months left. Perhaps not even sixty days."

"What are you trying to hand me?"

"The truth. And don't go looking for a silver platter underneath it, either."

"But I mind my own business. I don't hurt anybody. Why should I be in any danger?"

"Why does a government subsidy support one rental manager to sit here in this building every day—but ten guards to patrol it every night?"

Eric opened his mouth wide before shaping it for speech. "Who told you that?"

"Like I said, I know the setup." Wolzek crossed his legs, but he didn't lean back. "And in case you haven't guessed it, this is a business call, not a social one."

Eric sighed. "Might have figured," he said. "You're a Naturalist, aren't you?"

"Of course I am. We all are."

"Not I."

"Oh yes—whether you like it or not, you're a Naturalist, too. As far as the Yardsticks are concerned, everyone over three feet high is a Naturalist. An enemy. Someone to be hated, and destroyed."

"Think I'd believe that? Sure, I know they don't like us, and why should they? We eat twice as much, take up twice the space, and I guess when we were kids we gave a lot of them a hard time. Besides, outside of a few exceptions like ourselves, all the younger generation are Yardsticks, with more coming every year. The older people hold the key positions and the power. Of course there's a lot of friction and resentment. But you know all that."

"Certainly." Wolzek nodded. "All that and more. Much more. I know that up until a few years ago, no Yardstick held any public office or government position. Now they're starting to move in, particularly in Europasia. But there's so many of them now—adults, in their early twenties—that the pressure is building up. They're impatient, getting out of hand. They won't wait until the old folks die off. They want control now. And if they ever manage to get it, we're finished for good."

"Impossible!" Eric said.

"Impossible?" Wolzek's voice was a mocking echo. "You sit here in this tomb and when somebody tells you that the world you know has died, you refuse to believe it. Even though every night, after you sneak home and huddle up inside your room trying not to be noticed, ten guards patrol this place with subatomics, so the Yardstick gangs won't break in and take over. So they won't do what they did down south—overrun the office buildings and the factories and break them up, cut them down to size for living quarters."

"But they were stopped," Eric objected. "I saw it on the telescreen, the security forces stopped them—"

"Crapola!" Wolzek pronounced the archaicism with studied care. "You saw films. Faked films. Have you ever traveled, Eric? Ever been down south and seen conditions there?"

"Nobody travels nowadays. You know that. Priorities."

"I travel, Eric. And I know. Security forces don't suppress anything in the south these days. Because they're made up of Yardsticks now; that's right, Yardsticks exclusively. And in a few years that's the way it will be up here. Did you ever hear about the Chicagee riots?"

"You mean last year, when the Yardsticks tried to take over the synthetic plants at the Stockyards?"

"Tried? They *succeeded.* The workers ousted management. Over fifty thousand were killed in the revolution—oh, don't look so shocked, that's the right word for it!—but the Yardsticks won out in the end."

"But the telescreen showed—"

"Damn the telescreen! I know because I happened to be there when it happened. And if *you* had been there, you and a few million other ostriches who sit with your heads buried in telescreens, maybe we could have stopped them."

"I don't believe it. I can't!"

"All right. Think back. That was last year. And since the first of this year, what's happened to the standard size meat-ration?"

"They cut it in half," Eric admitted. "But that's because of Ag shortages, according to the telescreen reports—" He stood up, gulping. "Look here, I'm not going to listen to any more of this kind of talk. By rights, I ought to turn your name in."

"Go ahead." Wolzek waved his hand. "It's happened before. I was reported when I blasted the Yardsticks who shot my father down when he tried to land his jet in a southern field. I was reported when they killed Annette."

"Annette?"

"You remember that name, don't you, Eric? Your first girl, wasn't she? Well, I'm the guy who married her. Yes, and I'm the guy who talked her into having a baby without the benefit of Leff shots. Sure, it's illegal, and only a few of us ever try it any more, but we both agreed that we wanted it that way. A real, life-sized, normal baby. Or abnormal, according to the Yardsticks and the stupid government.

"It was a dirty scum of a government doctor who let her die on the table when he discovered the child weighed seven pounds. That's when I really woke up, Eric. That's when I knew there was going to be only one decision to make in the future—kill or be killed."

"Annette. She died, you say?"

Wolzek moved over and put his hand on Eric's shoulder. "You never married, did you, Eric? I think I know why. It's because you felt the way I did about it. You wanted a regular kid, not a Yardstick. Only you didn't quite have the guts to try and beat the law. Well, you'll need guts now, because it's getting to the point where the law can't protect you any more. The government is made up of old men, and they're afraid to take action. In a few years they'll be pushed out of office all over the world. We'll have Yardstick government then, all the way, and Yardstick law. And that means they'll cut us down to size."

"But what can you—we—do about it?"

"Plenty. There's still a little time. If we Naturalists can only get together, stop being just a name and become an organized force, maybe the ending will be different. We've got to try, in any case."

"The Yardsticks are human beings, just like us," Eric said, slowly. "We can't just declare war on them, wipe them out. It's not their *fault* they were born that way."

Wolzek nodded. "I know. Nothing is anybody's fault, really. This whole business began in good faith. Leffingwell and some of the other geniuses saw a problem and offered what they sincerely believed was a solution."

"But it didn't work," Eric murmured.

"Wrong. It worked only too well. That's the trouble. Sure, we eliminated our difficulties on the physical level. In less than thirty years we've reached a point where there's no longer any danger of overcrowding or starvation. But the psychological factor is something we can't cope with. We thought we'd ended war and the possibilities of war a long time ago. But it isn't foreign enemies we must fear today. We've created a nation divided into Davids and Goliaths—and David and Goliath are always enemies."

"David killed Goliath," Eric said. "Does that mean we're going to die?"

"Only if we're as stupid as Goliath was. Only if we wear our telescreens like invincible armor and pay no attention to the slingshot in David's hands."

Eric lit a reef. "All right," he said. "You don't have to lecture. I'm willing to join. But I'm no Goliath, really. I never had a fight in my life. What could I do to help?"

"You're a rental agent. You have the keys to this building. The guards don't bother you by day, do they? You come and go as you please. That means you can get into the cellars. You can help us move the stuff down there. And we'll take care of the guards some night, after that."

"I don't understand."

The friendly pressure on Eric's shoulder became a fierce grip. "You don't have to understand. All you do is let us plant the stuff in the cellars and let us get rid of the guards afterwards in our own way. The Yardsticks will do the rest."

"You mean, take over the building when it's not protected?"

"Of course. They'll take it over completely, once they see there's no opposition. And they'll remodel it to suit themselves, and within a month there'll be ten thousand Yardsticks sitting in this place."

"The government will never stand still for that."

"Wake up! It's happening all over, all the time, and nothing is being done to prevent it. Security is too weak and officials are too timid to risk open warfare. So the Yardsticks win, and I'm going to see that they win this place."

"But how will that help us?"

"You don't see it yet, do you? And neither will the Yardsticks. Until, some fine day three or four months from now, we get around to what will be planted in the cellars. Somebody will throw a switch, miles away, and—boom!"

"Wolzek, you couldn't—"

"It's coming. Not only here, but in fifty other places. We've got to fight fire with fire, Eric. It's our only chance. Bring this thing out into the open. Make the government realize this is war. Civil war. That's the only way to force them to take real action. We can't do it any other way; it's illegal to organize politically, and petitions do no good. We can't get a hearing. Well, they'll have to listen to the explosions."

"I just don't know—"

"Maybe you're the one who should have married Annette after all." Wolzek's voice was cold. "Maybe you could have watched her, watched her scream and beg and die, and never wanted to move a muscle to do anything about it afterwards. Maybe you're the model citizen, Eric; you and the thousands of others who are standing by and letting the Yardsticks chop us down, one by one. They say in Nature it's the survival of the fittest. Well, perhaps you're not fit to survive."

Eric wasn't listening. "She screamed," he said. "You heard her scream?"

Wolzek nodded. "I can still hear her. I'll always hear her."

"Yes." Eric blinked abruptly. "When do we start?"

Wolzek smiled at him. It was a pretty good smile for a man who can always hear screaming. "I knew I could count on you," he murmured. "Nothing like old friends."

"Funny, isn't it?" Eric tried to match his smile. "The way things work out. You and I being kids together. You marrying my girl. And then, us meeting up again this way."

"Yes," said Wolzek, and he wasn't smiling now. "I guess it's a small world."

10. Harry Collins—2032

Harry's son's house was on the outskirts of Washington, near what had once been called Gettysburg. Harry was surprised to find that it *was* a house, and a rather large one, despite the fact that almost all the furniture had been scaled down proportionately to fit the needs of a man three feet high.

But then, Harry was growing accustomed to surprises.

He found a room of his own, ready and waiting, on the second floor; here the furniture was of almost antique vintage, but adequate in size. And here, in an atmosphere of unaccustomed comfort, he could talk.

"So you're a physician, eh?" Harry gazed down into the diminutive face, striving to accept the fact that he was speaking to a mature adult. His own son—his and Sue's—a grown man and a doctor! It seemed incredible. But then, nothing was more incredible than the knowledge that he was actually here, in his child's home.

"We're all specialists in one field or another," his son explained. "Every one of us born and surviving during the early experimental period received our schooling under a plan Leffingwell set up. It was part of his conditional agreement that we become wards of the state. He knew the time might come when we'd be needed."

"But why wasn't all this done openly?"

"You know the answer to that. There was no way of educating us under the prevailing system, and there was always a danger we might be singled out as freaks who must be destroyed—particularly in those early years. So Leffingwell relied on secrecy, just as he did during his experimentation period. You know how *you* felt about that. You believed innocent people were being murdered. Would you have listened to his explanations, accepted the fact that his work was worth the cost of a few lives so that future billions of human beings might be saved? No, there was no time for explanation or indoctrination. Leffingwell chose concealment."

"Yes," Harry sighed. "I understand that better now, I think. But I couldn't see it then, when I tried to kill him." He flushed. "And I still can't quite comprehend why he spared me after that attempt."

"Because he wasn't the monster you thought him to be. When I pleaded with him—"

"*You* were the one!"

Harry's son turned away. "Yes. When I was told who you really were, I went to him. But I was only a child, remember that. And he didn't spare you out of sentimentality. He had a purpose."

"A purpose in sending me to prison, letting me rot all these years while—"

"While I grew up. I and the others like myself. And while the world outside changed." Harry's son smiled. "Your friend Richard Wade was right, you know. He guessed a great deal of the truth. Leffingwell and Manschoff and the rest of their associates deliberately set out to assemble a select group of nonconformists—men of specialized talents and outlooks. There were over three hundred of you at Stark Falls. Richard Wade knew why."

"And so he was dragged off and murdered."

"Murdered? No, Father, he's very much alive, I assure you. In fact, he'll be here tonight."

"But why was he taken away so abruptly, without any warning?"

"He was needed. There was a crisis, when Dr. Leffingwell died." Harry's son sighed. "You didn't know about that, did you? There's so much for you to learn. But I'll let him tell you himself, when you see him this evening."

Richard Wade told him. And so did William Chang and Lars Neilstrom and all the others. During the ensuing weeks, Harry saw each of them again. But Wade's explanation was sufficient.

"I was right," he said. "There was no Underground when we were at Stark Falls. What I didn't realize, though, was that there was an Overground."

"Overground?"

"You might call it that. Leffingwell and his staff formed the nucleus. They foresaw the social crisis which lay ahead, when the world became physically divided into the tall and the short, the young and the old. They knew there'd be a need of individuality then—and they *did* create a stockpile. A stockpile of the younger generation, specially educated; a stockpile of the older generation, carefully selected. We conspicuous rebels were incarcerated and given an opportunity to think the problem through, with limited contact with one another's viewpoints."

"But why weren't we told the truth at the beginning, allowed to meet face-to-face and make some sensible plans for the future?"

Harry's son interrupted. "Because Dr. Leffingwell realized this would defeat the ultimate purpose. You'd have formed your own in-group, as prisoners, dedicated to your own welfare. There'd be emotional ties—"

"I still don't know what you're talking about. What are we supposed to prepare for now?"

Richard Wade shrugged. "Leffingwell had it all planned. He foresaw that when the first generation of Yardsticks—that's what they call themselves, you know—came of age, there'd be social unrest. The young people would want to take over, and the older generation would try to remain in positions of power. It was his belief that tensions could be alleviated only by proper leadership on both sides.

"He himself had an important voice in government circles. He set up an arrangement whereby a certain number of posts would be assigned to people of his choice, both young and old. Similarly, in the various professions, there'd be room for appointees he'd select. Given a year or two of training, Leffingwell felt that we'd be ready for these positions. Young men, like your son, would be placed in key spots where their influence would be helpful with the Yardsticks. Older men such as yourself would go into other assignments—in communications media, chiefly. The skillful use of group-psychological techniques could avert open clashes. He predicted a danger-period lasting about twenty years—roughly, from 2030 to 2050. Once we weathered that span, equilibrium would be regained, as a second and third generation came along and the elders became a small minority. If we did our work well and eliminated the sources of prejudice, friction and hostility, the transition could be made. The Overground in governmental circles would finance us. This was Leffingwell's plan, his dream."

"You speak in the past tense," Harry said.

"Yes." Wade's voice was harsh. "Because Leffingwell is dead, of cerebral hemorrhage. And his plan died with him. Oh, we still have some connections in government; enough to get men like yourself out of Stark Falls. But things have moved too swiftly. The Yardsticks are already on the march. The people in power—even those we relied upon—are getting frightened. They can't see that there's time left to train us to take over. And frankly, I'm afraid most of them have no inclination to give up their present power. They intend to use force."

"But you talk as though the Yardsticks were united."

"They are uniting, and swiftly. Remember the Naturalists?"

Harry nodded, slowly. "I was one, once. Or thought I was."

"You were a liberal. I'm talking about the *new* Naturalists. The ones bent on actual revolution."

"Revolution?"

"That's the word. And that's the situation. It's coming to a head, fast."

"And how will we prevent it?"

"I don't know." Harry's son stared up at him. "Most of us believe it's too late to prevent it. Our immediate problem will be survival. The Naturalists want control for themselves. The Yardsticks intend to destroy the power of the older generation. And we feel that if matters come to a head soon, the government itself may turn on us, too. They'll have to."

"In other words," said Harry, "we stand alone."

"Fall alone, more likely," Wade corrected.

"How many of us are there?"

"About six hundred," said Harry's son. "Located in private homes throughout this eastern area. If there's violence, we don't have a chance of controlling the situation."

"But we can survive. As I see it, that's our only salvation at the moment—to somehow survive the coming conflict. Then, perhaps, we can find a way to function as Leffingwell planned."

"We'll never survive here. They'll use every conceivable weapon."

"But since there's no open break with the government yet, we could still presumably arrange for transportation facilities."

"To where?"

"Some spot in which we could weather the storm. What about Leffingwell's old hideout?"

"The units are still standing." Harry's son nodded. "Yes, that's a possibility. But what about food?"

"Grizek."

"What?"

"Friend of mine," Harry told him. "Look, we're going to have to work fast. And yet we've got to do it in a way that won't attract any attention; not even from the government. I suggest we set up an organizing committee and make plans." He frowned. "How much time do you think we have—a year or so?"

"Six months," his son hazarded.

"Four, at most," Wade said. "Haven't you been getting the full reports on those riots? Pretty soon they'll declare a state of national emergency and then nobody will be going anywhere."

"All right." Harry Collins grinned. "We'll do it in four months."

Actually, as it worked out, they did it in just a day or so under three.

Five hundred and forty-two men moved by jetter to Colorado Springs; thence, by helicopter, to the canyon hideaway. They moved in small groups, a few each week. Harry himself had already established the liaison system, and he was based at Grizek's ranch. Grizek was dead, but Bassett and Tom Lowery remained and they cooperated. Food would be ready for the 'copters that came out of the canyon.

The canyon installation itself was deserted, and the only problem it presented was one of rehabilitation. The first contingent took over.

The jetters carried more than their human cargo; they were filled with equipment of all sorts—microscans and laboratory instruments and devices for communication. By the time the entire group was assembled, they had the necessary implementation for study and research. It was a well-conceived and well-executed operation.

To his surprise, Harry found himself acting as the leader of the expedition, and he continued in this capacity after they were established. The irony of the situation did not escape him; to all intents and purposes he was now ruling the very domain in which he had once languished as a prisoner.

But with Wade and Chang and the others, he set up a provisional system which worked out very well. And proved very helpful, once the news reached them that open revolt had begun in the world outside.

A battered 'copter landed one evening at dusk, and the wounded pilot poured out his message, then his life's blood.

Angelisco was gone. Washington was gone. The Naturalists had struck, using the old, outlawed weapons. And it was the same abroad, according to the few garbled reports thereafter obtainable only *via* ancient shortwave devices.

From then on, nobody left the canyon except on weekly 'copter-lifts to the ranch grazing lands for fresh supplies. Fortunately, that area was undisturbed, and so were its laconic occupants. They neither knew nor cared what went on in the world outside; what cities were reported destroyed, what forces triumphed or went down into defeat, what activity or radioactivity prevailed.

Life in the canyon flowed on, more peacefully than the river cleaving its center. There was much to do and much to learn. It was, actually, a monastic existence, compounded of frugality, abstinence, continence and devotion to scholarly pursuits. Within a year, gardens flourished; within two years herds grazed the grassy slopes; within three years cloth was being woven on looms in the ancient way and most of the homespun arts of an agrarian society had been revived. Men fell sick and men died, but the survivors lived in amity. Harry Collins celebrated his sixtieth birthday as the equivalent of a second-year student of medicine; his instructor being his own son. Everyone was studying some subject, acquiring some new skill. One-time rebellious natures and one-time biological oddities alike were united by the common bond of intellectual curiosity.

It was, however, no Utopia. Some of the younger men wanted women, and there were no women. Some were irked by confinement and wandered off; three of the fleet of eleven 'copters were stolen by groups of malcontents. From time to time there would be a serious quarrel. Six men were murdered. The population dwindled to four hundred and twenty.

But there was progress, in the main. Eventually Banning joined the group, from the ranch, and under his guidance the study-system was formalized. Attempts were made to project the future situation, to prepare for the day when it would be possible to venture safely into the outside world once again and utilize newly-won abilities.

Nobody could predict when that would be, nor what kind of world would await their coming. By the time the fifth year had passed, even shortwave reports had long since ceased. Rumors persisted that radioactive contamination was widespread, that the population had been virtually decimated, that the government had fallen, that the Naturalists had set up their own reign only to fall victim to internal strife.

"But one thing is certain," Harry Collins told his companions as they assembled in the usual monthly meeting on the grounds before the old headquarters building one afternoon in July. "The fighting will end soon. If we hear nothing more within the next few months, we'll send out observation parties. Once we determine the exact situation, we can plan accordingly. The world is going to need what we can give. It will use what we have learned. It will accept our aid. One of these days—"

And he went on to outline a carefully-calculated program of making contact with the powers that be, or might be. It sounded logical and even the chronic grumblers and habitual pessimists in the group were encouraged.

If at times they felt the situation fantastic and the hope forlorn, they were heartened now. Richard Wade summed it up succinctly afterwards, in a private conversation with Harry.

"It isn't going to be easy," he said. "In the old science fiction yarns I used to write, a group like this would have been able to prevent the revolution. At the very least, it would decide who won if fighting actually broke out. But in reality we were too late to forestall revolt, and we couldn't win the war no matter on whose side we fought. There's just one job we're equipped for—and that's to win the peace. I don't mean we'll step out of here and take over the world, either. We'll have to move slowly and cautiously, dispersing in little groups of five or six all over the country. And we'll have to sound out men in the communities we go to, find those who are willing to learn and willing to build. But we can be an influence, and an important one. We have the knowledge and the skill. We may not be chosen to lead, but we can *teach* the leaders. And that's important."

Harry smiled in agreement. They *did* have something to offer, and surely it would be recognized—even if the Naturalists had won, even if the entire country had sunk into semi-barbarism. No use anticipating such problems now. Wait until fall came; then they'd reconnoitre and find out. Wait until fall—

It was a wise decision, but one which ignored a single, important fact. The Naturalists didn't wait until fall to conduct their reconnaissance.

They came over the canyon that very night; a large group of them in a large jetter.

And they dropped a large bomb....

---

11. Jesse Pringle—2039

They were after him. The whole world was in flames, and the buildings were falling, the mighty were fallen, the Day of Judgment was at hand.

He ran through the flames, blindly. Blind Samson. Eyeless in Gaza, treading at the mill. The mills of the gods grind slowly, but they grind exceedingly small.

Small. They were all small, but that didn't matter. They had the guns and they were hunting him down to his doom. Day of doom. Doomsday. The great red dragon with seven heads and ten horns was abroad in the land.

They had unleashed the dragon and his breath was a fire that seared, and his tail was a thunder that toppled towers. The dragon was searching him out for his sins; he would be captured and set to labor in the mill.

But he would escape, he must escape! He was afraid of them, small as they were, and great oaks from little acorns grow, it's the little things that count, and he dare not go a-hunting for fear of little men.

Jesse crouched against the dock, watching the grain-elevators burn. The whole city was burning, Babylon the mighty, the whole world was burning in God's final wrath of judgment.

Nobody believed in God any more, nobody read the Bible, and that's why they didn't know these things. Jesse knew, because he was an old man and he remembered how it had been when he was a little boy. A little boy who learned of the Word of God and the Wrath of God.

He could see the reflection of the flames in the water, now, and the reflection was shimmery and broken because of the black clusters floating past. Large clusters and small clusters. There were bodies in the water, the bodies of the slain.

Thunder boomed from the city behind him. Explosions. That's how it had started, when the Naturalists began blowing up the buildings. And then the Yardsticks had come with their weapons, hunting down the Naturalists. Or had it been that way, really? It didn't matter, now. That was in another country and besides, the wench was dead.

The wench *is* dead. His wench, Jesse's wench. She wasn't so old. Only seventy-two. But they killed her, they blew off the top of her head and he could feel it when they did. It was as if something had happened in *his* head, and then he ran at them and screamed, and there was great slaughter amongst the heathen, the forces of unrighteousness.

And Jesse had fled, and smote evil in the name of the Lord, for he perceived now that the time was at hand.

How the mighty are fallen.

Jesse blinked at the water, wishing it would clear, wishing his thoughts would clear. Sometimes for a moment he could remember back to the way things *really* were. When it was still a real world, with real people in it. When he was just a little boy and everybody else was big.

Strange. Now he was an old man, a big old man, and almost everybody else was little.

He tried to think what it had been like, so long ago. It was too long. All he could remember about being small was that he had been afraid. Afraid of the bigger people.

And now he was big, and afraid of the smaller people.

Of course they weren't real. It was just part of the prophecy, they were the locusts sent to consume and destroy. He kept telling himself there was nothing to fear; the righteous need not fear when the day of judgment is at hand.

Only somewhere inside of him was this little boy, crying, "Mama, Mama, Mama!" And somewhere else was this old man, just staring down into the water and waiting for them to find him.

Another explosion sounded.

This one was closer. They must be bombing the entire city. Or else it was the dragon, lashing his tail.

Somebody ran past Jesse, carrying a torch. No, it wasn't a torch—his hair was on fire. He jumped into the water, screaming, "They're coming! They're coming!"

Jesse turned and blinked. They were coming, all right. He could see them pouring out of the alleyway like rats. Rats with gleaming eyes, gleaming claws.

Suddenly, his head cleared. He realized that he was going to die. He had, perhaps, one minute of life left. One minute out of eighty years. And he couldn't fool himself any longer. He was not delirious. Day of judgment—that was nonsense. And there was no dragon, and these were not rats. They were merely men. Puny little men who killed because they were afraid.

Jesse was a big man, but he was afraid, too. Six feet three inches tall he was, when he stood up straight as he did now, watching them come—but he knew fear.

And he resolved that he must not take that fear with him into death. He wanted to die with something better than that. Wasn't there something he could find and cling to, perhaps some memory—?

A minute is so short, and eighty years is so long. Jesse stood there, swaying, watching them draw nearer, watching them as they caught sight of him and raised their weapons.

He scanned rapidly into the past. Into the past, before the time the wench was dead, back to when you and I were young, Maggie, back still earlier, and earlier, seeking the high point, the high school, that was it, the high school, the highlight, the moment of triumph, the game with Lincoln. Yes, that was it. He hadn't been ashamed of being six feet three inches then, he'd been proud of it, proud as he raised his arms and—

Splashed down into the water as the bullets struck.

And that was the end of Jesse Pringle. Jesse Pringle, champion basketball center of the Class of '79....

---

12. Littlejohn—2065

The helicopter landed on the roof, and the attendants wheeled it over to one side. They propped the ladder up, and Littlejohn descended slowly, panting.

They had a coasterchair waiting and he sank into it, grateful for the rest. Hardy fellows, these attendants, but then they were almost three feet tall. More stamina, that was the secret. Common stock, of course, but they served a purpose. Somebody had to carry out orders.

When they wheeled the coasterchair into the elevator, Littlejohn descended. The elevator halted on the first floor and he breathed a sigh of relief. Great heights always made him faint and dizzy, and even a short helicopter trip took its toll—the mere thought of soaring two hundred feet above the ground was enough to paralyze him.

But this journey was vital. Thurmon was waiting for him.

Yes, Thurmon was waiting for him here in the council chamber. The coasterchair rolled forward into the room and again Littlejohn felt a twinge of apprehension. The room was vast—too big for comfort. It must be all of fifty feet long, and over ten feet in height. How could Thurmon stand it, working here?

But he had to endure it, Littlejohn reminded himself. He was head of the council.

Thurmon was lying on the couch when Littlejohn rolled in, but he sat up and smiled.

"I greet you," he said.

"I greet you," Littlejohn answered. "No, don't bother to stay seated. Surely we don't need to be ceremonious."

Thurmon pricked up his ears at the sound of the unfamiliar word. He wasn't the scholarly type, like Littlejohn. But he appreciated Littlejohn's learning and knew he was important to the council. They needed scholars these days, and antiquarians too. One has to look to the past when rebuilding a world.

"You sent for me?" Littlejohn asked. The question was purely rhetorical, but he wanted to break the silence. Thurmon looked troubled as he replied.

"Yes. It is a matter of confidence between us."

"So be it. You may speak in trust."

Thurmon eyed the door. "Come nearer," he said.

Littlejohn pressed a lever and rolled up to the couchside. Thurmon's eyes peered at him through the thick contact lenses. Littlejohn noted the deep wrinkles around his mouth, but without surprise. After all, Thurmon was an old man—he must be over thirty.

"I have been thinking," Thurmon said, abruptly. "We have failed."

"Failed?"

Thurmon nodded. "Need I explain? You have been close to the council for many years. You have seen what we've attempted, ever since the close of the Naturalist wars."

"A magnificent effort," Littlejohn answered politely. "In less than thirty years an entire new world has risen from the ruins of the old. Civilization has been restored, snatched from the very brink of a barbarism that threatened to engulf us."

"Nonsense," Thurmon murmured.

"What?"

"Sheer nonsense, Littlejohn. You're talking like a pedant."

"But I *am* a pedant." Littlejohn nodded. "And it's true. When the Naturalists were exterminated, this nation and other nations were literally destroyed. Worse than physical destruction was the threat of mental and moral collapse. But the Yardstick councils arose to take over. The concept of small government came into being and saved us. We began to rebuild on a sensible scale, with local, limited control. The little community arose—"

"Spare me the history lesson," said Thurmon, dryly. "We rebuilt, yes. We survived. In a sense, perhaps, we even made certain advances. There is no longer any economic rivalry, no social distinctions, no external pressure. I think I can safely assume that the danger of future warfare is forever banished. The balance of power is no longer a factor. The balance of Nature has been partially restored. And only one problem remains to plague mankind."

"What is that?"

"We face extinction," Thurmon said.

"But that's not true," Littlejohn interrupted. "Look at history and—"

"Look at us." Thurmon sighed. "You needn't bother with history. The answer is written in our faces, in our own bodies. I've searched the past very little, compared to your scholarship, but enough to know that things were different in the old days. The Naturalists, whatever else they might have been, were strong men. They walked freely in the land, they lived lustily and long.

"Do you know what our average life-expectancy is today, Littlejohn? A shade under forty years. And that only if one is fortunate enough to lead a sheltered existence, as we do. In the mines, in the fields, in the radioactive areas, they die before the age of thirty."

Littlejohn leaned forward. "Schuyler touches on just that point in his *Psychology of Time*," he said, eagerly. "He posits the relationship between size and duration. Time is relative, you know. Our lives, short as they may be in terms of comparative chronology, nevertheless have a subjective span equal to that of the Naturalists in their heyday."

"Nonsense," Thurman said, again. "Did you think that is what concerns me—whether or not we feel that our lives are long or short?"

"What then?"

"I'm talking about the basic elements essential to survival. I'm talking about strength, stamina, endurance, the ability to function. That's what we're losing, along with the normal span of years. The world is soft and flabby. Yardstick children, they tell us, were healthy at first. But *their* children are weaker. And their grandchildren, weaker still. The effect of the wars, the ravages of radiation and malnutrition, have taken a terrible toll. The world is soft and flabby today. People can't walk any more, let alone run. We find it difficult to lift and bend and work—"

"But we won't have to worry about such matters for long," Littlejohn hazarded. "Think of what's being done in robotics. Those recent experiments seem to prove—"

"I know." Thurmon nodded. "We can create robots, no doubt. We have a limited amount of raw materials to allocate to the project, and if we can perfect automatons they'll function quite adequately. Virtually indestructible, too, I understand. I imagine they'll still be able to operate efficiently a hundred or more years from now—if only they learn to oil and repair one another. Because by that time, the human race will be gone."

"Come now, it isn't that serious—"

"Oh, but it is!" Thurmon raised himself again, with an effort. "Your study of history should have taught you one thing, if nothing else. The tempo is quickening. While it took mankind thousands of years to move from the bow and arrow to the rifle, it took only a few hundred to move from the rifle to the thermonuclear weapon. It took ages before men mastered flight, and then in two generations they developed satellites; in three, they reached the moon and Mars."

"But we're talking about *physical* development."

"I know. And physically, the human race altered just as drastically in an equally short span of time. As recently as the nineteenth century, the incidence of disease was a thousandfold greater than it is now. Life was short then. In the twentieth century disease lessened and life-expectancy doubled, in certain areas. Height and weight increased perceptibly with every passing decade. Then came Leffingwell and his injections. Height, weight, life-expectancy have fallen perceptibly every decade since then. The war merely hastened the process."

"You appear to have devoted a great deal of time to this question," Littlejohn observed.

"I have," answered the older man. "And it is not a question. It is a fact. The one fact that confronts us all. If we proceed along our present path, we face certain extinction in a very short time. The strain is weakening constantly, the vitality is draining away. We sought to defeat Nature—but the Naturalists were right, in their way."

"And the solution?"

Thurmon was silent for a long moment. Then, "I have none," he said.

"You have consulted the medical authorities?"

"Naturally. And experiments have been made. Physical conditioning, systems of exercise, experimentation in chemotherapy are still being undertaken. There's no lack of volunteers, but a great lack of results. No, the answer does not lie in that direction."

"But what else is there?"

"That is what I had hoped you might tell me," Thurmon said. "You are a scholar. You know the past. You speak often of the lessons of history—"

Littlejohn was nodding, but not in agreement. He was trying to comprehend. For suddenly the conviction came to him clearly; Thurmon was right. It was happening, had happened, right under their smug noses. The world was weakening. It was slowing down, and the race is only to the swift.

He cursed himself for his habit of thinking in platitudes and quotations, but long years of study had unfitted him for less prosaic phraseology. If he could only be practical.

Practical.

"Thurmon," he said. "There is a way. A way so obvious, we've all overlooked it—passed right over it."

"And that is—?"

"Stop the Leffingwell injections!"

"But—"

"I know what you'll say. There have been genetic mutations. Very true, but such mutations can't be universal. A certain percentage of offspring will be sound, capable of attaining full growth. And we don't have the population-problem to cope with any more. There's room for people again. So why not try it? Stop the injections and allow babies to be born as they were before." Littlejohn hesitated before adding a final word, but he knew he had to add it; he knew it now. "Normally," he said.

Thurmon nodded. "So that is your answer."

"Yes. I—I think it will work."

"So do the biologists," Thurmon told him. "A generation of normal infants, reared to maturity, would restore mankind to its former stature, in every sense of the word. And now, knowing the lessons of the past, we could prepare for the change to come. We could rebuild the world for them to live in, rebuild it psychically as well as physically. We'd plan to eliminate the rivalry between the large and the small, the strong and the weak. It wouldn't be difficult because there's plenty for all. There'd be no trouble as there was in the old days. We've learned to be psychologically flexible."

Littlejohn smiled. "Then that *is* the solution?" he asked.

"Yes. Eliminating the Leffingwell injections will give us a good proportion of normal children again. *But where do we find the normal women to bear them?*"

"Normal women?"

Thurmon sighed, then reached over and placed a scroll in the scanner. "I have already gone into that question with research technicians," he said. "And I have the figures here." He switched on the scanner and began to read.

"The average nubile female, aged thirteen to twenty-one, is two feet, ten inches high and weighs forty-eight pounds." Thurmon flicked the switch again and peered up. "I don't think I'll bother with pelvic measurements," he said. "You can already see that giving birth to a six or seven-pound infant is a physical impossibility under the circumstances. It cannot be done."

"But surely there must be *some* larger females! Perhaps a system of selective breeding, on a gradual basis—"

"You're talking in terms of generations. We haven't got that much time." Thurmon shook his head. "No, we're stopped right here. We can't get normal babies without normal women, and the only normal women are those who began life as normal babies."

"Which comes first?" Littlejohn murmured. "The chicken or the egg?"

"What's that?"

"Nothing. Just an old saying. From history."

Thurmon frowned. "Apparently, then, that's all you can offer in your professional capacity as an historian. Just some old sayings." He sighed. "Too bad you don't know some old prayers. Because we need them now."

He bowed his head, signifying the end of the interview.

Littlejohn rolled out of the room.

His 'copter took him back to his own dwelling, back across the rooftops of New Chicagee. Ordinarily, Littlejohn avoided looking down. He dreaded heights, and the immensity of the city itself was somehow appalling. But now he gazed upon the capital and center of civilization with a certain morbid affection.

New Chicagee had risen on the ashes of the old, after the war's end. Use of thermo-nucs had been limited, fortunately, so radioactivity did not linger, and the vast craters hollowed out by ordinary warheads had been partially filled by rubble and debris. Artificial fill had done the rest of the job, so that now New Chicagee was merely a flat prairie as it must have been hundreds of years ago—a flat prairie on which the city had been resurrected. There were almost fifty thousand people here in the capital; the largest congregation of population on the entire continent. They had built well and surely this time, built for the security and certainty of centuries to come.

Littlejohn sighed. It was hard to accept the fact that they had been wrong; that all this would end in nothingness. They had eliminated war, eliminated disease, eliminated famine, eliminated social inequality, injustice, disorders external and internal—and in so doing, they had eliminated themselves.

The sun was setting in the west, and long shadows crept over the city below. Yes, the sun was setting and the shadows were gathering, the night was coming to claim its own. Darkness was falling, eternal darkness.

It was quite dark by the time Littlejohn's 'copter landed on the rooftop of his own dwelling; so dark, in fact, that for a moment he didn't see the strange vehicle already standing there. Not until he had settled into his coasterchair did he notice the presence of the other 'copter, and then it was too late. Too late to do anything except sit and stare as the gigantic shadow loomed out of the night, silhouetted against the sky.

The shadow shambled forward, and Littlejohn gaped, gaped in terror at the titanic figure. He opened his mouth to speak, but words did not form; there were no words to form, for how does one address an apparition?

Instead, it was the apparition which spoke.

"I have been waiting for you," it said.

"Y-yes—"

"I want to talk to you." The voice was deep, menacing.

Littlejohn shifted in his coasterchair. There was nowhere to go, no escape. He gazed up at the shadow. Finally he summoned a response. "Shall we go inside?" he asked.

The figure shook its head. "Where? Down into that dollhouse of yours? It isn't big enough. I've already been there. What I have to say can be said right here."

"W-who are you?"

The figure stepped forward, so that its face was illuminated by the fluorescence streaming from the open door which led to the inclined chairway descending to Littlejohn's dwelling.

Littlejohn could see the face, now—the gigantic, wrinkled face, scarred and seared and seamed. It was a human face, but utterly alien to the humanity Littlejohn knew. Faces such as this one had disappeared from the earth a lifetime ago. At least, history had taught him that. History had not prepared him for the actual living presence of a—

"Naturalist!" Littlejohn gasped. "You're a Naturalist! Yes, that's what you are!"

The apparition scowled.

"I am not a Naturalist. I am a man."

"But you can't be! The war—"

"I am very old. I lived through your war. I have lived through your peace. Soon I shall die. But before I do, there is something else which must be done."

"You've come here to kill me?"

"Perhaps." The looming figure moved closer and stared down. "No, don't try to summon help. When your servants saw me, they fled. You're alone now, Littlejohn."

"You know my name."

"Yes, I know your name. I know the names of everyone on the council. Each of them has a visitor tonight."

"Then it is a plot, a conspiracy?"

"We have planned this very carefully, through the long years. It's all we lived for, those few of us who survived the war."

"But the council wasn't responsible for the war! Most of us weren't even alive, then. Believe me, we weren't to blame—"

"I know." The gigantic face creased in senile simulation of a smile. "Nobody was ever to blame for anything, nobody was ever responsible. That's what they always told me. I mustn't hate mankind for multiplying, even though population created pressure and pressure created panic that drove me mad. I mustn't blame Leffingwell for solving the overpopulation problem, even though he used me as a guinea-pig in his experiments. I mustn't blame the Yardsticks for penning me up in prison until revolution broke out, and I mustn't blame the Naturalists for bombing the place where I took refuge. So whose fault was it that I've gone through eighty years of assorted hell? Why did I, Harry Collins, get singled out for a lifetime of misery and misfortune?" The huge old man bent over Littlejohn's huddled form. "Maybe it was all a means to an end. A way of bringing me here, at this moment, to do what must be done."

"Don't harm me—you're not well, you're—"

"Crazy?" The old man shook his head. "No, I'm not crazy. Not now. But I *have* been, at times, during my life. Perhaps we all are, when we attempt to face up to the complications of an average existence, try to confront the problems which are too big for a single consciousness to cope with in a single life-span. I've been crazy in the city, and crazy in the isolation of a cell, and crazy in the welter of war. And perhaps the worst time of all was when I lost my son.

"Yes, I had a son, Littlejohn. He was one of the first, one of Leffingwell's original mutations, and I never knew him very well until the revolution came and we went away together. He was a doctor, my boy, and a good one. We spent almost five years together and I learned a lot from him. About medicine, but that wasn't important then. I'm thinking of what I learned about love. I'd always hated Yardsticks, but my son was one, and I came to love him. He had plans for rebuilding the world, he and I and the rest of us. We were going to wait until the revolution ended and then help restore sanity in civilization.

"But the Naturalists flew over and dropped their bomb, and my boy died. Over four hundred of our group died there in the canyon—four hundred who might have changed the fate of the world. Do you think I can forget that? Do you think I and the few others who survived have ever forgotten? Can you blame us if we did go crazy? If we hid away out there in the western wilderness, hid away from a world that had offered us nothing but death and destruction, and plotted to bring death and destruction to that world in return?

"Think about it for a moment, Littlejohn. We were old men, all of us, and the world had given us only its misery to bear during our lifetimes. The world we wanted to save was destroying itself; why should we be concerned with its fate or future?

"So we changed our plans, Littlejohn. Perhaps the shock had been too much. Instead of plotting to rebuild the world, we turned our thoughts to completing its destruction. Our tools and texts were gone, buried in the rubble with the bodies of fine young men. But we had our minds. Crazed minds, you'd call them—but aware of reality. The grim reality of the post-revolutionary years.

"We burrowed away in the desert. We schemed and we dreamed. From time to time we sent out spies. We knew what was going on. We knew the Naturalists were gone, that six-footers had vanished from a Yardstick world. We knew about the rehabilitation projects. We watched your people gradually evolve new patterns of living and learning. Some of the former knowledge was rescued, but not all. Our little group had far more learning than you've ever dreamed of. Fifty of us, between ourselves, could have surpassed all your scientists in every field.

"But we watched, and we waited. And some of us died of privation and some of us died of old age. Until, at last, there were only a dozen of us to share the dream. The dream of destruction. And we knew that we must act swiftly, or not at all.

"So we came into the world, cautiously and carefully, moving unobtrusively and unobserved. We wanted to contemplate the corruption, seek out the weaknesses in your degenerate civilization. And we found them, immediately. Those weaknesses are everywhere apparent, for they are physical. You're one of a dying race, Littlejohn. Mankind's days are numbered. There's no need for grandiose schemes of reactivating warheads in buried missile-centers, of loosing thermo-nucs upon the world. Merely by killing off the central council here in New Chicagee, we can accomplish our objective. A dozen men die, and there's not enough initiative left to replace them. It's as simple as that. And as complicated."

Harry Collins nodded. "Yes, as complicated. Because the only weaknesses we've observed *are* physical ones. We've seen enough of the ways of this new civilization to realize that.

"All of the things I hated during my lifetime have disappeared now—the crowding, the competition, the sordid self-interest, the bigotry, intolerance, prejudice. The anti-social aspects of society are gone. There is only the human race, living much closer to the concept of Utopia than I ever dreamed possible. You and the other survivors have done well, Littlejohn."

"And yet you come to kill us."

"We came for that purpose. Because *we* still retained the flaws and failings of our former cultures. We looked for targets to blame, for villains to hate and destroy. Instead, we found this reality.

"No, I'm not crazy, Littlejohn. And I and my fellows aren't here to execute revenge. We have returned to the original plan; the plan Leffingwell had, and my son, and all the others who worked in their own way for their dream of a better world. We come now to help you. Help you before you die—before we die."

Littlejohn looked up and sighed. "Why couldn't this have happened before?" he murmured. "It's too late now."

"But it isn't too late. My friends are here. They are telling your fellow council-members the same thing right now. We may be old, but we can still impart what we have learned. There are any number of technological developments to be made. We can help you to increase your use of atomic power. There's soil reclamation and irrigation projects and biological techniques—"

"You said it yourself," Littlejohn whispered. "We're a dying race. That's the primary problem. And it's an insoluble one. Just this afternoon—" And he told him about the interview with Thurmon.

"Don't you understand?" Littlejohn concluded. "We have no solution for survival. We're paying the price now because for a while we wouldn't heed history. We tried to defeat Nature and in the end Nature has defeated us. Because we would not render unto Caesar the things which are—"

Harry Collins smiled. "That's it," he said.

"What?"

"Caesar. That's the answer. Your own medical men must have records. I know, because I learned medicine from my son. There used to be an operation, in the old days, called a caesarean section—used on normal women and on dwarfs and midgets too, in childbirth. If your problem is how to deliver normal children safely, the technique can be revived. Get hold of some of your people. Let's see what data you have on this. I'll be glad to furnish instruction—"

There was excitement after that. Too much excitement for Littlejohn. By the time the council had assembled in emergency session, by the time plans were formulated and he returned to his own dwelling in the helicopter, he was completely exhausted. Only the edge of elation sustained him; the realization that a solution had been found.

As he sank into slumber he knew that he would sleep the clock around.

And so would Harry Collins. The old man and his companions, now guests of the council, had been temporarily quartered in the council-chambers. It was the only structure large enough to house them and even so they had to sleep on the floor. But it was sufficient comfort for the moment.

It was many hours before Harry Collins awoke. His waking was automatic, for the tiny telescreen at the end of the council room glowed suddenly, and the traditional voice chirped forth to interrupt his slumber.

"Good morning," said the voice. "It's a beautiful day in New Chicagee!"

Harry stared at the screen and then he smiled.

"Yes," he murmured. "But tomorrow will be better."

THE END

Milton Keynes UK
Ingram Content Group UK Ltd.
UKHW031049120324
439302UK00006B/470

9 789357 946650